APART

APART

R.P. MacIntyre

AND

Wendy MacIntyre

GROUNDWOOD BOOKS
HOUSE OF ANANSI PRESS
TORONTO BERKELEY

Groundwood Books / House of Anansi Press
110 Spadina Avenue, Suite 801, Toronto, Ontario M5V 2K4

Distributed in the USA by Publishers Group West
1700 Fourth Street, Berkeley, CA 94710

We acknowledge for their financial support of our publishing program the Canada Council for the Arts, the Government of Canada through the Book Publishing Industry Development Program (BPIDP) and the Ontario Arts Council.

ONTARIO ARTS COUNCIL
CONSEIL DES ARTS DE L'ONTARIO

Library and Archives Canada Cataloguing in Publication
MacIntyre, R.P.
Apart / R.P. MacIntyre and Wendy MacIntyre
ISBN-13: 978-0-88899-750-0 (bound).–
ISBN-10: 0-88899-750-7 (bound).–
IBSN-13: 978-0-88899-834-7 (pbk.)–
ISBN-10: 0-88899-834-1 (pbk.)
I. MacIntyre, Wendy. II. Title.
PS8575.I67A73 2007   jC813'.54   C2007-902025-9

Cover illustration by Martin O'Neill
Design by Michael Solomon
Printed and bound in Canada

To Jane MacIntyre and Annie Poirier

The authors would like to thank
editor Shelley Tanaka
for her kind and thorough diligence, and,
as humbly as possible, each other,
without whose effort and belief
this work would not exist.

July 17

Dear Whoever at Box 4893:

For starters I don't read the *Globe and Mail* every day. I never read it. If you asked me a week ago what it was, I wouldn't know. But it's funny what you end up reading while you're waiting to have your teeth pulled. Okay, tooth. Just one. In the back, one of those you don't need, apparently, that grows in sideways and pushes everything else out of whack.

Anyway, enough about my teeth.

I had to write you about the guy with the tattoo on his arm. I think I seen him. Actually, I think I know him but maybe there's more than one guy with that kind of tattoo and that kind of streaky hair who rides a black '86 ElectraGlide. A very cool bike, by the way.

I take it you are a girl because only a girl would talk about her Missing Father. No guy I know would care if his dad disappeared, and he would not call him "father" unless he was from Shaunavon Heights which is a ritzy high-rent hood near here filled with Beemers and Porsches — and brand new ElectraGlide Hogs belonging to doctors and lawyers before they get ripped off by real bikers — like maybe your dad. Or Father, as you call him.

If, on the other hand, you're a guy, get a life, buddy! Just eat it. We can't all have our daddies, you know.

Whoever you are, the real reason I'm writing is because if this dude is your father, you don't want anything to do with him and you should be happy he's not around messing up your life.

So long,

James Charles MacSween

P.S. About my name. My dad calls me James, my mom calls me Charles, and my friends call me Sween.

Dear James Charles MacSween:

You know how sometimes words lift off the page and fill your head with a good kind of light? Well, that's how it felt when I read your letter.

It's just so great to hear from somebody who has seen my father (more on why I use that word later) and knows where he is. In your letter you sound like a really honest guy. So I'm presuming you aren't jerking me around and making it up about seeing him. Don't get offended. I believe I can trust you because of the way you write. You wouldn't start off by telling me about your experience at the dentist if your letter was just some mean joke.

You wouldn't believe what a relief it is to get a letter from somebody who sounds normal. I had no idea so many perverts and weirdos read the *Globe and Mail* and buy stamps. Or is there just something about the words tattoo, blond stripe and bike that trigger a sick response in certain people? Some of the answers I got were so gross I had to rip them in little pieces and flush them.

So thanks a lot, James Charles MacSween, for giving me some hope here and sounding like a genuine person.

I am really hoping you can help me some more because I am getting desperate. If I was alone, I couldn't care less if I never saw my pretty-boy father again. I call him Father because Dad sounds too warm. Father is a word that helps me keep him separate in my head. I can't explain this very well. It's like a way of staying formal and cold, so that Father is something over in the corner you don't have to deal with.

I need him to come home for my mom's sake. She has been drinking herself stupid since he left — straight vodka, no mix, glugging it down like it's water. She also has a supply of little bright blue pills that she is very good at hiding. Picture a soggy paper bag with legs. That is the state she has got herself in, and I can't stand it.

I love her, and I don't want to see her kill herself with booze and pills.

There's another selfish reason I have for wanting my father to come back, and that's my little brother, Timmy, who doesn't talk. He needs a lot of care because he's hyperactive and right now it's up to me to look after him all the time because my mom is so completely out of it.

I don't mind now so much because it's summer. But in September I want to go back to school. This is super-extra-extraordinarily important to me because it will be my last year before university. I have to do really well so that I can get a scholarship.

So those are the reasons I want that jerk to come home.

APART

So my mom will pull herself together, and so Timmy won't be just my responsibility 24/7.

I need help.

Could maybe get a letter to him? You say that you *think* you know him. What does that mean? I guess we ought to make sure this really is my father we're both talking about.

So here are some more details. He has a piece missing from his left ear lobe that some woman bit off in a really personal situation except I'm not supposed to know that. He calls himself Gunner, or sometimes The Gunner when he is feeling really full of himself. But his real first name is Archibald. I probably shouldn't tell you that. If you are talking to him, don't ever call him Archibald or you will be back at your dentist having little bloody stumps pulled out of your mouth. I am deadly serious.

A last identifying detail I hate to mention. When he left he was with a peroxide blonde in too-tight clothes named Gloria. This woman is the original slut-o-rama.

I am sending you this book of stamps so that it won't cost you anything to write back and tell me if we are talking about the same guy. And you can tell me then what you mean by saying I should be happy he isn't around. Is he into something else besides bikes and his great big ego? Whatever he is up to, I have to know.

What I'm counting on is that real love has deep roots. My mom still loves him, and he loved her once. Won't he still have the roots of that love somewhere inside him?

You don't have to answer that.

I wish I had a computer so I could e-mail you, but maybe you don't have one either. Our phone has been cut off here so even if I knew your number I couldn't call you.

I am really hoping to hear from you soon.

Thanks a lot again.

Jessica Doig

P.S. What is a Beemer?

Dear Jessica:

I'm not sure what you mean by a good kind of light, even if I'm not jerking you around about your dad.

Anyway, it's not him — the guy I thought might be. In the first place, his name is not Gunner or Archibald either. His name is Gerry and he's a grease-monkey. His snake tattoo isn't shedding. It's just slithering. He has both his ears.

I also asked him if he had a daughter named Jessica.

He laughed and said, "Not to my knowledge. Why do you ask?"

I mumbled something about a friend wanting to know.

"Well, maybe. Is her mother hot?"

Of course I said I didn't know, I never met you. And he laughed some more. "Ask her if she wants DNA samples."

So, do you?

He does have a girlfriend named Gloria, but she is not blonde — peroxide or otherwise. She's got short black hair and rides a Softail. She's from around here and is the big sister of a guy at school.

I'm sorry to disappoint you on the one hand, but glad it's

not him on the other because he is a real jerk — although it sounds like your real dad is no picnic. I take it your mom is not in real great shape either. (A paper bag with legs? Wow!) With parents like that, how come you sound so sane? The chicks I know with deadbeat dads and strung-out moms are basket-cases themselves. Even me, with the perfect parents and perfect little sister as well as a dog (Zamboni) is considered a basket-case by pretty well everyone in my life, especially grade twelve teachers but including said parents and sister — AND dog, who growls at me when I yell at Suzanne (my sister).

But you must be kidding about your little brother. His name is really Timmy? As in Tiny Tim? As in the David Copperfield or whatever the name of that guy is? Just whose idea was that? It's bad enough he's retarded or whatever, but to have to live with a handle like that is too much. Poor guy.

Anyway, I'm returning the stamps. I think I can afford the postage but I appreciate the thought.

I'm glad your question about love wasn't one you wanted me to answer because I know nothing about it. In fact, I really don't believe in it. I think it's a figment of someone's imagination. Someone in Hollywood or Nashville who figured out a way to make money by selling soppy movies or songs. If it exists, I sure don't know what it looks like or feels like. Chicks, or girls or women or whatever you want to be called (excuse me for being so P.I. here) have never shown any interest in me anyway.

Just read that over. Yes, I'd like a little cheese with my whine.

APART

Don't know why I told you all that. Anyway, this letter is probably a disappointment to you. Good luck finding your father.

So long,

Sween

P.S. A Beemer is a BMW, as in Bavarian Motor Works, as in expensive car or bike.

Dear Sween:

Thanks for writing back, and for sending back the stamps.

Yes, I was disappointed — very disappointed — to find out that the man you thought might be my father is some knucklehead grease-monkey named Gerry. In fact I was more than disappointed. I was hopping mad. I mean, super-extra-extraordinarily mad — the way you get when all your hope comes tumbling down, and you're back to Square One, or Square Zero.

So I did what I always do in these situations. I shook my fist in the air and I hopped up and down. (I can't yell because that upsets my mom who wakes up and thinks Timmy has sat on a lit burner on the stove again.)

Timmy doesn't care much for yelling either. He screws up his face and starts to blare when there's any noise he isn't used to. But my silent hopping-mad dances make him laugh and clap his hands, which is great, because Timmy doesn't laugh very often. And when his face looks lit-up and happy, I feel a hundred times better and get hopeful again.

I wonder if you are reading this and thinking, "What a wacko!" Lots of people, especially kids my age, think I should be locked up in a padded room. I'm used to it. So go ahead and think it too if you like, James Charles MacSween. I don't care what you or anybody else thinks.

Actually, that's not totally true. You were nice enough to write twice and to check out this creepy Gerry guy. And you know about the word chick being P.I. and most guys would think caring about vocabulary is just a load of B.S.

In fact, you sound like a sensitive, thoughtful person. I think you write very well too, and I am sure you will meet some girl who appreciates your qualities. I suppose now I sound like your old auntie who knits you ugly socks every Christmas. But I mean it, Sween. You're okay. Don't put yourself down. That's a very dangerous practice and I know of what I speak.

About love — I'll be honest, I don't know either. I mean, I don't know anything about intimate feelings, reciprocated or otherwise, for members of the opposite sex. Most of the guys at school are crude and cruel. The only exceptions are the guys who are gay, and they have even more trouble than I do.

I do know about love for Timmy, and it's real mother-bear stuff. He gets lots of strange looks from people who should know better, and the little shits (pardon my language) in town throw rocks at him and call him The Dummy. I really want to keep him safe.

I love my mom because she is my mom, and I know she'll get on her feet some day. This week she was a bit better. She looked in the mirror and said, "God, I look like hell!" and that's always a good sign, for a while, anyway. At least she is up and moving, putting on her make-up and breathing some fresh air. Definitely less soggy and less paper-baggy.

Needless to say, we haven't heard anything from The Almighty Gunner. If Mom could just get used to the idea that he has gone for good, we could all move on and get a grip.

It really made me laugh when you asked how come I sound so sane. Well, one answer is Timmy. (And by the way, I think it's a good name, and it's *A Christmas Carol* and not *David Copperfield* that has Tiny Tim as a character.) He needs a protector, and right now that's me. He's not retarded. He's autistic, which means he's kind of locked into a world of his own. Sometimes he just sits on the floor and hugs himself and rocks back and forth, and he can do that for hours.

I think things must be pretty scary sometimes inside Timmy's head, and that's why he needs to comfort himself with that kind of rocking motion. That's why it's so great too, when something breaks through — like my stupid hopping-mad dance — that makes him laugh.

The other big answer to what keeps me sane is my Great-Grandma Doig. She came over from Scotland many years ago, but she still has her accent and plenty of great stories. She calls me her braw wee lassie, which means she thinks I'm all right although I'm certainly not wee. (She uses a lot of really neat Scots words like dree and dreich and sleekit.)

I know Doig doesn't sound like a Scottish name, but it is, part of the Clan Drummond. The Doigs originally came from *Macbeth* country. Did you ever study it in school? I love that play.

Reading keeps me sane too. I've got books from Great-

Grandma Doig I must have read ten times — books that came over with her on the boat, like Robert Louis Stevenson's *Kidnapped* and *A Child's Garden of Verses*, and that one's not as sucky as the title makes it sound.

Great-Grandma Doig told me that when she first came to Canada she was so homesick for Scotland, she would have walked back over the North Atlantic if there had been a bridge. I want to go there some day and see all the places she's told me about.

I hope that answers your question about the roots of my sanity, and thanks for your interest.

I think Zamboni is a great name for a dog, by the way. We used to have a kitten but Timmy had a habit of hugging it a bit too tightly, so we had to give it away before he squeezed the life right out of it. There's a big moose that shows up in the backyard every once in a while, though.

Thanks for clearing up what a Beemer is. The Gunner used to specialize in fixing up antique bikes. I grew up surrounded by pieces of old Indians and Nortons. I liked the Triumph Bonneville the best. Very elegant. Personally, I am not very partial to Hogs.

So long, Sween. I hope you get all the good wine and cheese and friendly squeezes you deserve, and sooner rather than later.

Yours truly,

Jessica

September 5

Dear Jess:

I hope you don't mind me calling you that. I almost feel like we're old buds now in spite of the fact that I'm really surprised to hear back from you. I thought that once I didn't know your old man that'd be it. Finito. But I can't say I'm really disappointed in hearing from you. The opposite in fact, for a couple of reasons. The most important of which is at this very moment it looks like I'm working real hard at my in-class writing assignment in LA. We have to describe something — anything — and out here on the bald prairie that is a problem because there's nothing to describe except maybe the sky hanging up there like a great big blue flag from one end of the earth to the other, with the sun poking though like God's bellybutton.

Bellybuttons were banned at our school. Yours? I kind of liked them, although I no longer have the urge to blow raspberries onto some chick's tummy the way you do to a little kid, like I actually used to do to Suzanne when she was a baby and I was about six. She would giggle and so would I. I don't dare touch her any more though or she goes wailing to my mom.

APART

Speaking of little sisters — do you have any, or just Tim? BTW, thanks for including those weird drawings he made. They are truly strange and look more like runic writing or whatever than pictures of any kind. Did he copy them from somewhere, or make them up by himself?

Anyway, I was also really interested in your grandma's language. Maybe she knew my grandma. They speak the same thing! Except, unlike you I don't remember any of the words. And now, of course, it's too late because she died last year. I don't even know where she was from. Some island somewhere. Barra? Near there anyway. I think. I'll have to ask my dad even though it's like he chose to forget where his family was from. He is not a great fund of knowledge about such things. And my mom is no different. She thinks her ancestors came from France, but isn't real sure. I used to sometimes get called chink or Indian at school because of my eyes that arc sort of slanted. It really makes you wonder about your past.

Glad to hear that your mom is looking at the mirror again. I never thought of that before, but it makes sense if you care what other people think of you. You got to care for yourself a bit anyway. Not that I spend hours in front of the mirror, but I know guys who do.

I look long enough to make sure I don't have anything stuck to my teeth.

Teeth. I hate teeth. No, I hate MY teeth. They want to put wires in my mouth and straighten them out. I want to leave them parked where God put them (not that I'm a religious freak or anything) but if my chiclets are bent a little bit, so what? I'm not going to be a movie star or anything. Who cares!? In the olden days, people just lived with what they had in their mouths, right?

So, if you ever see a picture of me, I'm the one smiling with his mouth closed. Maybe I'll send you a school picture when they come out and if it's not too ugly.

Why am I talking about my teeth? I'll shut up.

I really want to talk about YOU. What gets you all excited — aside from Tim? (Sorry BTW about calling him a retard. I looked up autistic on the web. Whew! Heavy.) Sorry for calling you sane too. You've got to be a little bit crazy to accept your situation the way you do.

Your heart must be at least as big as the prairie sky.

And what do you look like?

Please don't tell me you have red hair. I have this image of you that includes that — LONG red hair that you only occasionally let down. And you have an open wide face with bright blue eyes. No, they're brown. Am I anywhere close to right? Write? Are you like your writing?

I got to say a word about your writing style. It's so…what's the word? Proper, or something. Mature? I'm sure the Hack would love it. (Mr. Hackles is our LA teacher. He wants us all to become "litter it.") That is not a put-down by the way, just an observation. I wish I could be so…Poised. That's it. I imagine you as a very poised person, like your writing. I'm all over the place, like a balloon you let go of and it farts bounding off the walls and ceiling, then lies on the floor flat and dead.

Bell's ringing.

APART

• • •

It's a few hours later and I'm finishing this up at home. My folks have sort of vanished for the evening. They go to "staff functions" at the university where Dad teaches.

Remember I peed all over those people who live in Shaunavon Heights with Beemers and Hogs in their driveways? Well, I'm one of them. My life has been handed to me on a silver platter. Nothing is hard. I get everything I want. I'm smart. I do good at school (I know it should be, "I do *well* at school." I sometimes make mistakes on purpose just to prove I'm a real person.)

You don't have to do that. You have poise in the middle of disaster.

I envy you.

Sincerely,

Sween

September 19

Dear Sween:

I have to tell you that I thought very hard about not writing back to you at all. To put it mildly, I was pissed off to learn about the sudden turn in your lifestyle, or at least in the way you presented yourself. And then you made it even worse with all that junk about my so-called "poise."

Why did you pretend in your first letter that you were from the kind of home where they've never heard of the *Globe and Mail*? In your house, it sounds as if even the dog has his own subscription. Don't tell me! Zamboni is studying Ancient Greek with the help of a special study light you fixed up in his doghouse.

Just think about it from my point of view. What if I suddenly told you that I am actually a kinky pork butcher who wants to develop a special relationship with a young person? Do you see what I mean?

I don't mean I think you are in any way like a perverted pork butcher. It's just that I felt kind of shocked. No, more than that. I felt extra-extraordinarily betrayed by your belated revelation that you come from the land of the shiny

Beemers and Hogs. (And have you ever noticed how often people who are well off live in places called The Heights? They just want to emphasize, I suppose, that the rest of us live down below.)

So here's another up-front confession. I am terribly envious of *you*. I am super-extra-extraordinarily envious of the fact you have a computer and an Internet connection, a father who teaches at university (what does your mother do?), a normal, healthy little sister, and a phone (or probably phones) that works. Oh, and no big pile of Final Reminder unpaid bills from utility companies on the kitchen table beside your mother's overflowing ashtray. I'll bet your parents go jogging every morning in matching track suits, right?

That's it. Finito, as you say. My heart definitely isn't at least as big as the prairie sky, as you put it.

Take a piece of paper and stick the tip of your pen through it. Look at the ragged little hole you've made and that's about the size of my metaphorical heart. I have had some pretty mean thoughts about people in my time, and not just that The Gunner would fall off his bike and break his damn leg. Again. He's already done that. Maybe his neck then.

Then there are the unpleasant thoughts I have about certain girls at school who pretended they liked me and wanted to know me and asked sympathetic questions about Timmy. It turned out all they wanted was to meet my drop-dead gorgeous father. Or they wanted me to get them a photograph of him, and they would be really specific, like, "In full gear, standing beside his Hog" or "bare-chested." Ugh! And when I didn't do it, they got really nasty and called me and my mother some very ugly names. This happened three separate times, before I wised up.

Did you ever read Margaret Atwood's *Cat's Eye*? That book was a big comfort to me because I saw that this kind of nastiness and cruelty is a lot more common among teenage girls than most people like to believe. I suppose I mean than *I* like to believe, and that's just my gullibility showing again.

I already told you that lots of kids think I'm weird. Well, make that *all* kids. I am your classic outcast loner. This is definitely not a gripe. In fact, I like it this way because I just don't care about the things other kids do — which movie star has the best hair or the nicest behind or the cutest nose, or what's the coolest thing to say, or wear, or watch on TV.

My Great-Grandma Doig says I have an old soul. And I really do prefer being with old people, rather than kids my own age.

And by the way, the words my great-grandma uses (like dreich and sleekit) are Scots words. Scots is what happened to the English language north of the border between England and Scotland. I think maybe the language your grandma spoke might be Gaelic, especially if she came from one of the islands in the Hebrides.

Dreich means dreary, in case you are wondering. When you use this word about the weather, it means wet and dismal, which it often is in this part of New Brunswick. Sleekit is a great adjective for The Gunner because it means a person who is very charming and smooth on the surface, but a real creep underneath.

And here's one of Great-Grandma's sayings I really love, and that helps keep me going. "You have to dree your weird, child," she tells me. That means you have to endure your fate. And I have quite a lot of fate to endure.

Oh, and I want to say how super pleased I was that you checked out autism on the Internet, and that you liked Timmy's drawings. Actually, I think they are his attempt to imitate writing because he sees me doing a lot of that.

Did you notice how much repetition there is in the shapes he makes? He really loves order and the same way of doing things at exactly the same time every day. He hates any kind of change in his routine, or in the arrangement of things in his room.

There have been some big changes in his life and mine since I last wrote to you.

Remember I told you that one of the reasons I wanted The Gunner to come back was so Mom would pull herself together and help look after Timmy? Otherwise I didn't see how I could go back to school this term.

Well, come the first week of school, Mom had a major pills-and-booze relapse, triggered by the visit of a "friend" who told her that she heard The Gunner and Gloria had set up house together in Halifax.

Not what Mom needs to hear. Anyway, she was a complete mess after that, and I couldn't leave either her or Timmy.

Then we got a visit from one of my teachers, Mr. Powys,

whom I really like because he is so encouraging about my writing and my ideas. He wanted to know why I hadn't shown up for class.

What I didn't know is that his wife is a social worker and she pulled some strings and got Timmy into a day class at a place where they work with kids with special needs. He has been going there for a week now, and so far it is amazing how well it is working out because he doesn't seem to mind going. And I am back at school, trying to get good enough marks so I have a chance at the scholarship I need so desperately.

Maybe because things are better for Timmy, my mom seems to be back on track for now. She is even talking about going back to work. She is a beautician. She and Gloria used to work together at the same salon, which is another reason I think she has been slow to get back to it.

So I am keeping my fingers crossed here, especially for Timmy because his one experience at regular school a few years ago was not a roaring success. Well, maybe roaring is the right word. They sent him home after half a day when he pulled one of his wild tantrums. Timmy can really howl and be loudly unruly, and he is terrifically strong for a little kid. They tried to hold him down, and he hates that. So his kindergarten teacher ended up with some pretty bad bruises.

You asked if I have any sisters. No, there is just me and Timmy.

I think Timmy's problems are one of the reasons things started to go wrong between Mom and The Gunner.

Basically, The Gunner is ashamed of Timmy. He just says, "Put him away where he belongs."

Do you see why I hate my father so much? Timmy belongs right here, not some warehousey institution where they throw away the key!

Sorry about yet another rant. I have to stop writing soon as it is time for Timmy's bedtime story. Needless to say, he always wants the same one or two, which can get a bit tedious for me.

Oh yes, you asked what "excites" me. Books. Poetry. The idea of writing really well myself, in a fresh way that makes people sit up and notice, and maybe getting published. I love art too. Once, I went on a school trip to Fredericton and the art gallery there was amazing. The Beaverbrook Gallery — doesn't that just sound beautiful? There was a little painting called "Lady Macbeth Sleepwalking" by a French artist named Delacroix. It was exquisite but at the same time, the image made my scalp prickle because it showed her blood-stained and distraught after Duncan's murder.

What else excites me? The idea of seeing the world. Scotland is first on my list, but I also want to see Paris and Venice and China and even Tibet, if that is ever possible — the Himalayas.

That's it, Sween, except to put you straight on your idea that I have long red hair. In fact, it's black and coarse, like The Gunner's, minus his dyed skunk stripe. My hair is very long, down past my hips, so usually it's in a long braid. You are right about the brown eyes, though.

I'm not pretty, although Great-Grandma Doig says I've got a face with a lot of character. In other words, my nose is more beak than button, and my cheekbones are wide and stick out a bit too much.

On the subject of sticking out, I am sure your teeth are probably fine, Sween. I've noticed that people who are well off have a thing about getting braces for their kids' teeth. If you were poor, I bet no one would think you needed them at all.

In any case, thanks a lot for saying that you almost feel like we're old buds. That meant a lot to me, even if after reading this letter, you don't feel it any more.

Take care of yourself, Sween. You are a good guy for sure, and I thought the image of the prairie sun sticking through the sky like God's bellybutton was awesome. I certainly wouldn't have thought of *that*.

With a lot of respect,

Jessica

Dear Jess:

This is my third attempt at answering your letter. I'm not sure how to begin. At first I was ticked off that you were ticked off. Then I just felt totally useless and hypocritical and I threw your letter away. Then I had to dig it out of the garbage, knock the coffee grounds off and try to explain.

I'll begin with this:

Sorry.

I was just trying to be honest, to set the record straight, to let you know exactly what (who) you're dealing with. If my memory serves me, I never claimed that my home never heard of the *Globe and Mail* — just that I didn't read it. In point of fact, my fascist father reads the *National Post* and considers the *Globe* a socialist rag. He won't allow it in the house. If I happen to stumble across it, like I did in the dentist's office, I read it. Or parts of it, like the Personals.

Yes, I did make the impression that I do not live where I do (at the moment) but I didn't know then that we would still be communicating now. Again, I'm just trying to set the record straight and be honest. Well, as honest as I can be.

Sometimes it's hard to tell what the truth is. It seems to vary a lot from person to person. My dad for instance (who calls me Smartass 90 percent of the time) believes a whole lot of things are true that I think are complete shit.

We do not get along, my dad and I.

In fact I don't get along with a lot of people. People in authority. I have what is referred to as an attitude. I don't like being told what to do. So consequently I often don't do what I'm told. This has got me kicked out of three schools in the last two years. One more and Dad says I can "move the hell out, go live on the street if you just want to do what you want."

I might, too.

I hate to see you pick on Zamboni. He's just a dog. A not very smart dog at that. We often call him Boni (as in bony because he studies whatever it is that dogs study when they snuffle up to your crotch). Anyway, if Greek's what he smells there, then I guess he's studying it. I somehow doubt it. If you and I behaved like Zamboni in public, we'd be in jail.

Shaunavon Heights are in fact on high ground. And yes, they do look down on the rest. I hate where I come from. That's why I tried to hide it. Don't get me started. DO NOT be envious of me for any reason — least of all my Internet connection, my fascist university professor father and my doormat mother. He says jump and she says how high. She lives in some sort of lobotomized 1950's time-warp.

My sister Suzanne is developing the worst traits of both my parents. She's hardly thirteen and she's planning the SHAPE of her wedding cake, the exact pastel shade of her bridesmaids' gowns and where she's going on her honeymoon. (Majorca, she says. She can't even spell it, much less know where it is.) All this, and she's never even been on a date!

And no, my parents do not have matching jogging suits. Dad is out of shape — well, in the shape of a pear — and Mom's in the shape of a celery stick. She takes Pilotes (sp?) or yoga that require spandex and mats she carries rolled up under her skinny arm. And yes, they're both reformed smokers. That's about all they have in common — except their matching beige leathers for when they go riding on dad's bike. You cannot imagine anything more pathetic. Beige leathers.

But no, I don't want your unpaid bills or your mom's ashtray either. That sounds like no fun at all.

But hey! I did that experiment you mention with pen through paper — murdering good bond to show the dimensions of your heart. What a tough gal you are! Being ticked off by chicks who want to eat your old man's ear! That's funny! I would have been more inclined to put that pencil somewhere else. On the other hand, what can you really do? I've had guys lusting after my spandexed mom. She has a good body too (if you like thin) and likes to show it off. I don't get particularly upset. I just shake my head. I mean really. There's no explaining lust. I've seen Zamboni try to hump a cat. Wrong species, Boni!! There's lots of people like my dog.

Are you really gullible? Or just a wishful thinker? I personally think that you're just a good person (and smart too — way smarter than me) and just can't believe how stupid some people can be. That's not gullibility, that's choosing not to go there, choosing the high road, as your grandmother would probably say — except she'd say it in Scots. She'd remind you again of your "old soul" and that would be that. What a great concept! Along with "dreich" and "sleekit." Those friends of yours sound pretty sleekit to me.

I'm not entirely sure about dreeing your fate. If that means accepting your lot in life, I'm against it. That's what my mom has done and what my little sister is doing. What most of the planet seems to be doing. There must be some point where you have to say, "Enough! I'm not putting up with this anymore!" I just barely keep grovelling along, "Yes sir, No sir." Dad likes it when I call him Sir.

We're going to have to agree to disagree on Margaret Atwood. I read *Cat's Eye* for a class assignment. What an ordeal. I can't stand her. Or maybe it was just Risley. (Ridley? Rigley?) Why didn't she just slit her throat — I mean if her childhood was so terrible? I think she liked whining more than she liked living. And then all this painting the Virgin Mary stuff. Give me a break. There was something very showy-offy about it. Snobby. Lookit how smart I am. Anyway, that's my Margaret Atwood experience.

Sorry.

I'm glad Timmy seems to like school and that you do too. I wish I could say the same. I am so fed up with school, the prison and its guards it's all I can do to remain civil to the teachers that I can tolerate (Hacks being one) and almost impossible to be nice to those who are out and out jerks.

APART

What is the best you can hope for Timmy? Could he ever work or live on his own? I guess what I'm really wondering is can he live without you? It seems to me that you are the string that's holding a lot of things together. Better you than me, girl. That's why I admire you. As far as writing goes, there's no doubt in my mind that you'll do it one day.

Travel excites me too, but I don't have much desire to see other countries — except maybe Scotland. I want to see this country, Canada, all of it. I want to trudge through the snow in Inuvik, hike through the cedars of B.C. and lie on the red sands of Prince Edward Island. And maybe get out to New Brunswick to see a friend of mine some day. A brown-eyed girl with hair down past her waist!

Really?! That is long.

So your face has "character," eh? That's what you call cheekbones and nose. You don't paint a real flattering picture of yourself. You're probably just being modest. And yes, my refusing braces is causing all sorts of grief around here. The rich are different from you and I, someone said. Yeah, they wear braces.

Again, I'm sorry I made you mad. I need someone I can open up to who isn't going to try and fix me. I'm not broken. I'm just trying to be me. I'm not always very good at it because I'm not always sure of who me is. So I make mistakes. I also sometimes think that me isn't a very nice person, and I don't like him much. But I'm working on it.

Hope you don't mind the picture I'm including. As you can see, Zamboni has character too. At least he smiles with his mouth open. What you can't see in the picture is that I'm almost six feet tall. And yes, my hair is growing back. With winter coming on, I need all the warmth I can get.

I look forward to hearing from you. Sometimes the time drags between these letters.

Sincerely,

Sween

October 17

Dear Sween:

First off, I am really sorry to hear about your trouble at home. And I apologize for being flippant about Zamboni and the Ancient Greek. I did not mean to pick on him, as you say. Sometimes my pen runs faster than my brain, and I can't stop it.

Zamboni looks like a good and noble companion. He has great lugs (that's Scots for ears).

I like the photograph. It means a lot to be able to picture you in my mind. It's great to hear that your hair is growing back, though. Some people are afflicted with baldness, and they deserve our sympathy. (Don't you think afflicted is just the most extra-extraordinarily descriptive word? You can just picture people going around with boulders on their backs, or huge stones in their pockets or shoes. Or shiny bare heads in the freezing cold world.)

I suppose the shaved head has the advantage of dramatizing your eyes. They are very striking. They probably help you to see through all the B.S. in this world.

What you said about truth varying from person to person

shook me up a bit because I have been thinking about this a lot recently. Believe me, The Gunner and I don't agree on many things, including Timmy's chances to learn to talk and read.

My father and I don't even agree about what's funny. The Gunner thinks dirty jokes are cute, and that going to strip clubs is "just a bit of fun."

Little Miss Tightass, he used to call me. Is that better or worse than being called Smartass?

Wouldn't it be great if we both had sensitive, supportive, understanding fathers?

And wow! I didn't know women like your mom existed anymore. Doesn't she do volunteer work at a library or an animal shelter or something? But it is good that she is keeping in shape.

I am sure your little sister will outgrow the wedding cake fantasy. Lots of people want at least one big production number in their lives, and a lot of girls get sucked into the lie that the white wedding will be the most astounding thing that ever happens to them.

It all looks like fluff and window dressing from where I stand. It seems to me the "perfect wedding" dream is just feeding a great big fat industry — like the one you mentioned feeding Nashville and Hollywood. It gives a lot of people work, like caterers and chauffeurs and wedding planners and dressmakers and the people who write and take photographs for *Bride* magazine.

Probably this is just a stage your sister is going through.

It's maybe just part of the deep-down desire everybody has to be the star of the show. When I was a quite a bit younger than your sister, I dreamed of being a ballerina. There were photographs in an old magazine of Great-Granny's that really made an impression on me when I was a kid. They showed this extra-extraordinarily glamorous ballerina (Margot somebody?) dancing with a man whose name I don't remember except that he was Russian. (He had eyes kind of like yours, Sween.)

Anyway, she looked so amazingly strong and beautiful, with her black hair pulled back tightly from her face, and a perfect profile.

I wanted to be like her, but of course there was never any money for ballet lessons, which are in pretty short supply anyway in this part of N.B. Having feet the size of small battleships (The Gunner is right on this one) didn't help.

But for about a year I spent a lot of time daydreaming about pirouetting on the points of my satin slippers, rising in the air and floating into the arms of my handsome Russian partner, getting standing ovations and heaps of red roses flung at my feet. (In my daydreams, my feet are NOT battleships.)

I outgrew that one. So there's hope for your sister too.

I want to say something really serious now, Sween, and that is that I think you should try to stick it out and put up with what all those dumb people in authority want. I really do know it's tough. I may make it sound as if I love every class in school, but it's really Mr. Powys that keeps me going.

What I hate most are the people who talk to me like I'm an idiot just because I'm younger, or maybe because they know my family is poor and about Timmy, and that The Gunner has a certain "reputation." I hate it with a passion, because I know I'm smarter than they are. That's not arrogance. I really do know it. Okay, maybe I have a bit of pride too.

What I do with these blockheads is bite my tongue and put up with it. I know it's tough when what you are burning to do is talk back. But I tell myself that if I endure it now, I will be super extraordinarily and gloriously free later. If we can tough it out now, in a year or two we will be able to spring ourselves right over and far, far beyond all their pitiful pointed little heads.

I hope you can try to endure it, Sween. Because from what I've heard from kids who have tried it, it really is grim out there on the street.

Also, I know a lot more about poverty than you do, and I am not trying to talk down to you here. It is no fun at all being cold for days at a time because your parents don't have money to pay the fuel bill, or wanting to have a good wash but there's no hot water because the electricity has been cut off. Or stuffing layers of paper inside your shoes to help stop the wet coming through the holes in your soles because you can't afford new ones.

I know you are tall, and that would probably help. But from what I've heard, there are thousands of creeps out there on the street.

I know kids who got hooked on some really nasty drugs when they decided to live on the street. Out there, it's easy to get hooked by all kinds of horrible things, and sometimes there's no way back. I know kids from around here who decided they wanted to see the West Coast and managed to hitch across the country. Two of them ended up hooking and junked-out in Vancouver. One of them is dead now.

If you can just put up with your dad and school for another year, once you're in university and away from home, you can be and say what you want. You could get a job — like being a writer — where you can be your own boss. You might not have a lot of money, but you won't be under anybody's thumb. That's my dream, anyway.

And here's something else you could try, Sween (you might think this is absolutely wacko, but I'm going to tell you anyway). You might want to think about getting a spirit animal to help you endure the crap. I mean a kind of imaginary helper, like the mice that help Cinderella, or the amazing cat in Puss-in-Boots.

I can imagine you rolling your eyes, but I am not kidding here. Maybe you've already had a dream about your animal guide. I suppose yours would have to be a creature that would get along with Zamboni, because I think dogs sense when there are spirits around.

I've never told anyone but Timmy this before. My spirit animal is a black bear. I had a really startling dream once about being chased by a bear, but then suddenly I was the bear, and I was running faster and more powerfully than I could ever do in real life. It was the kind of running that is almost like flying.

When I woke up, I was perfectly happy, as if there was a radiant light in my head, and in my whole body. That dream made me feel a lot more positive about things. Because I get really down sometimes, and my bear spirit helps me get through the dark thoughts. We run together toward the light.

Think about it, Sween. This idea is not as crazy as it sounds. Okay, it *is* as crazy as it sounds. But sometimes being what the straight arrows and pointy heads call crazy is a super extraordinary way of surviving the garbage.

That's one of the reasons I love Macbeth. Even though I know he is a murderer made mad by his ambition, you have to admire his staying power. When he knows the game is up, he says, "No, I don't want to die in a cowardly way like a Roman on my own sword. I'm going to go down fighting."

Don't get me wrong. I hate violence. I can't watch movies with a lot of violence, or even some of the things they show on the TV news.

But the thing you have to love about Macbeth is the way he toughs it out to the very end. And I think that's like me and my spirit bear. That's what we have to do. Tough it out through all the black bits till we see the light we're heading for.

I haven't told you my best news, and that is that Timmy is swimming and he loves it. There is a community pool his teacher takes the kids to, and Timmy is apparently a natural.

We just didn't know because we never took him swimming.

I've gone to watch him and he is like a little dolphin. He can swim with his head right under the water. And he loves it. He looks really happy. And I am extra happy for him because I can't swim at all. I love to look at the ocean, but I get absolutely terrified if my feet can't touch the bottom when I do go wading in the water at Baie-des-Chaleurs, for example.

To answer your questions about Timmy's future, I believe anything is possible. Once his vocabulary gets bigger, he can turn some corners. He has some amazing gifts I haven't told you about. But I have to stop writing soon. So telling you about them can wait for next time.

The photo of me and Timmy is a bit overexposed because Great-Grandma Doig took it and she's not very good with the camera. The Gunner said we look like ghosts and I got the feeling that's what he would prefer. And sometimes the feeling's mutual.

Let's both try to dree it with all the pointy-heads, Sween. Freedom's just around the corner.

Don't let them get you down.

Affectionately,

Jessica

November 2

Dear Jess:

Don't worry about my trouble at home. Whatever happens,
I'll survive. It does get boring though and I sometimes just
feel like packing up and leaving. Problem is, for where?

Last week my dad got a half million dollars for a research
grant for the department he works for (Crop Sciences) to
develop some new kind of genetically modified wheat. Does
he thank anybody? No, he screams, "They're robbing me!
How can I do my job when they throw peanuts at me?!"

I said, "So give them to me."

He got up like he was going to hit me. But I stood up. I'm
now taller than my dad and he must have thought twice because
he just stared me in the eye and said, "You are such a smartass."

I left. I went for a long walk.

In the first place, genetically modified anything is a big question mark in my books. In the second place, $500,000 is a lot of
money. I could do a lot with that kind of cash. I bet you could
too. It'd probably set up Timmy for quite a while and get him
the best of what he needs to take some of the pressure off you.

When I go for a walk, it's by the river where you always

run into some wildlife — usually just birds like magpies but sometimes deer or beavers. That day there was a coyote — right here in town. I've never seen one up close before. He looked me right in the eye, sort of like my dad did, but wasn't threatening me at all. At any rate, there was a "moment" there, like the one you describe with your black bear.

I swear he smiled at me. Like he found me really amusing. Then he padded off into the bush. So if I have an animal spirit, that's the one I'd like. Sometimes things are just so miserable you have to laugh. I think that's what Coyote was telling me.

My father is such a fool.

No need either to apologize for Zamboni. You did make me laugh out loud by describing him as a "good and noble companion." He barks a good line, but when the chips are down, he's nowhere to be found. He is COWARD DOG. He cries under the bed when it thunders. He barks at spiders. He chases birds. Yes, he does have great lugs. Too bad he can't hear with them. Really, he's pretty well deaf.

When I get depressed or feel down on myself, I have a habit of cutting all my hair off — with the dog's clippers. My hair's pretty well grown back now and seems darker than it was before. It used to be fairly blond, but not any more. Whatever you do, don't cut YOUR hair. It is stunningly beautiful. (And you're not too bad yourself — for sure not all nose and cheeks.)

Your father and mine sound like flip sides of the same bad coin. What a pair of complete jerks. They should get together. Except you know what? They'd hate each other. The only thing they have in common are a pair of asses, you and me — Smart and Tight. Ha! The one thing I can't see my old man doing is running off with Gloria, or someone like her. Why would he? He's got my mom who still looks good in leather pants and who waits on him hand and foot. That's her volunteer work. Although I suppose Dad would claim she gets paid for it.

I don't know about your father, but my father thinks he is sensitive, supportive and understanding. He thinks everything in our relationship is my problem. Maybe he's right. I can be a total jerk too. The difference is I'm willing to admit it.

I'm doing my best to endure the blockheads, idiots, power trippers and general asses that seem to be in control of my life. It's getting harder and harder to go to class. School shouldn't have to be something you endure.

Don't worry about me being taken up by some kind of meat peddler. Nor would I ever become a drug addict because I'm just not interested. Smoking is a bad enough addiction and before you start ragging on me, I'm working on giving it up. (Not soon enough according to my dad. Another reason we don't get along — the one legitimate reason.) I drink the occasional brew, but nothing like most guys.

I kind of liked that you liked the unlikable Macbeth (did that make sense?) for all the WRONG reasons. You have an original (but slightly demented) mind. Going down swinging is a good character trait in normal circs, but not when it's to hang onto power. I didn't like him at all. (No reflection on you.) What he did to McDuff's children was too much. Him I liked. A big, dumb, tough soldier who called his kids his pretty chickens. You knew Macbeth wasn't long for the world after that.

Winter's coming on. I can stand the cold and snow, but I hate the dark. I've got an old car I call The Beast, that gets really cantankerous with the dropping temperature. For some reason Dad doesn't let me park it in the garage (God knows, we've got enough room). I guess he doesn't want oil dripping all over the floor, but that he lets it be seen outside on the driveway by everyone who passes by surprises me. It is several different shades of rust and looks more like a calico cat than a car.

It might not be much but it's a kind of symbol of my freedom. I don't have to depend on anyone for a ride. Sometimes I just want to get in and drive — forever. Trouble is, I'm not quite sure how far The Beast would get. Ah, well. Better than a kick in the arse, as my Uncle Jerry would say.

I haven't mentioned Uncle Jerry. He's the only sane member in the family. He must be. He's been barred from the house for three or four years now. But every now and then he calls me and we sneak out for a coffee. Uncle Jerry is Dad's "bad" brother. He was a dentist, but lost his license because of some very dumb things he did with drugs and patients. He's done time in prison and now works as a janitor, cleaning offices. Including dentists' offices. He thinks it's funny, as in ironic. I don't know if you'd like him, but at least he's real.

Hey, you take care. Of yourself, as well as Timmy.

As always, your prairie friend,

Sween

Dear Sween:

I am so happy about your meeting with the coyote. That's amazing that he was right there in the city where you happened to be walking.

This is the kind of big coincidence — right after I wrote you about my spirit bear — that gets me really excited. Sometimes I think coincidences are one of the ways that another world (I mean the mysterious spirit world that is mostly invisible to us) suddenly shows itself in this "real" day-to-day, dirty, full-of-problems place we live.

Do you know what I mean? It's like right out of the blue you get an amazing glimpse of this totally other place where there's a super extra-extraordinary look to the light, and time feels different and the wind smells sweet, and you really think you could fly and animals can speak, and you are so perfectly happy there are simply no words equal to the feeling.

Anyway, I think maybe ecstasy comes close to being the right word for this feeling. I just looked it up in my dictionary and it comes from the Ancient Greek for "standing outside yourself." And that really fits in with what I feel at those moments — like I am right outside my physical body.

Maybe you think I'm totally nuts here. I know The Gunner does.

"Come down to earth, Jessica," he used to tell me, in the days when he still spoke more than three words to me at a time. "Life's a bitch and the sooner you face up to that the easier it's going to be for you. It's a nasty world out there, got it? And that's all there is. No fairy land. No la-la land. Not like your stupid storybooks. Am I getting through, Jessica? Try and concentrate on studying for the kind of job that will make you some big bucks. Like a stockbroker or something."

The Gunner is always impressed by people who have the "big bucks," even if he secretly despises them because he thinks he's the one who should be rich.

Anyway, those are the only words of fatherly advice I ever got from The Gunner. What a cretin! Well, I don't believe him. I don't believe that the common-sense everyday world we see is all there is, and that the most important thing in life is to make a lot of money. But what can you expect from a man who's spent most of his life enthralled with machines made of metal and rubber that go fast, and with the look of his own precious mug in the mirror?

Enough about that jerk.

I think it's great that you've found an animal spirit guide who has a sense of humor. Here in N.B. the Maliseet people call the trickster in their legends Glooskap. We had an Elder come into the school one day to talk to us about Maliseet culture. I remember his Glooskap liked to fart a lot, and he was very fond of making fools of other creatures who were pompous know-it-alls.

I don't know if my spirit bear appreciates that kind of fooling around. He seems like the kind of bear who would read heavy-duty philosophy while sitting on the john. He strikes me as an eminently serious bear.

Come to think of it, our spirit animals probably don't need to read anything at all. They already know everything that matters.

We just have to believe in them and respect them.

And I bet your calico car is just the kind of vehicle Coyote loves to ride in, with his head hanging out the window and his mouth open tasting the night air.

But you're right. It is really weird that your dad doesn't mind everyone seeing The Beast parked outside your house. Do you think maybe he had a car like that when he was your age? Shaunavon Heights can't be as snobby as I'd imagined, or they would have got a petition going by now to have your Beast put down.

The idea of anybody getting a grant for half a million dollars just boggles my mind. If someone gave my mom even five hundred dollars right now, she would probably leap up and do several cartwheels in a row. (She can, too. She is still very slim and flexible. And she does a cartwheel every year on her birthday. That's on April 1 so it's quite a few months off, but I am hoping she will carry on this tradition even if His Mightiness is not around to see.)

Did you know that the GM seeds they sell to developing countries grow plants from which you can't harvest seed to plant again? In other words, people who are already extremely poor have to buy new seed every year from the GM seed manufacturers, who probably all own Beemers and jacuzzis and lotus-scented swimming pools.

So the whole GM enterprise sounds like Big-Pig Capitalistic Greed to me.

Maybe your dad's research will lead him to see the light, and he'll recognize the Frankenplants for the super extraordinarily huge mistake they are.

Your Uncle Jerry certainly sounds like he's been right around the Wheel of Fortune. But he must be a strong and bounce-back kind of guy if he can appreciate the irony in his situation. And I am glad you have a friend in your family somewhere.

Our situation at home has changed a bit because Mom has started dating a guy named Lancelot (no kidding) Beauchemin. To be honest, I don't know whether this is a good thing or not.

She is looking really pretty again though. When she's looking after herself, my mom is the kind of woman you look at and immediately think of flowers.

Anyway, Lancelot Beauchemin is obviously very taken with my mom and he is also quite a good mechanic. We have an old, super extraordinarily cantankerous car too, and it's comforting to know someone could help us get it going if it conks out, which it often does. Lancelot actually manages a used car lot in Bathurst so I guess you could say he is a legitimate business person.

The problem is I know that Mom is still smitten with The Gunner, and in terms of physical attractiveness, Lancelot is just not in my father's league. He has a little pot belly starting and his hair has begun to recede pretty badly. And he has the kind of features that aren't very memorable, if you know what I mean.

I know it is extraordinarily colossally unfair to judge someone on the basis of appearance, and I'm not intending to put Lancelot down. It's just I'm presuming that in this whole complicated, super weird business of sexual attraction and love, looks do matter.

I mean, I happen to have parents who are both extremely good-looking and that must be one of the reasons they were drawn to each other in the first place.

So I really don't know if Lancelot has a hope of replacing The Gunner. There are nights when I can hear Mom crying in her room. I can't tell you how hopeless and sad that makes me feel.

But she is being brave — not boozing too much or gobbling pills, and she's never late for work at the salon.

Sometimes I wonder if all the upheaval and anguish and turmoil and toing and froing people go through for the sake of love-based-in-sex can really be worth it. I've been thinking a lot about what Hamlet says to Ophelia: "Get thee to a nunnery!" and the idea of that kind of safe, no-guys-allowed place really appeals to me. No fuss. No muss. No tears.

I don't want to end up like my mom, needing some jerk like The Gunner as badly as a drug addict needs a fix.

Back to the nunnery idea. I guess that deep down I still

want somewhere safe to take Timmy and look after him myself. I know this is an absolutely crazy idea but I still fear he is going to be hurt and wrenched out of shape, even by people with the best intentions.

Some of the autistic kids who have been in the special needs class a lot longer than Timmy behave in ways I'm not that happy about. I think maybe the teachers concentrate too much on getting the kids to look and behave as "normal" as possible so they don't stick out so much.

When I went to see Timmy swimming, for example, I was introduced to two of the other kids. The teaching assistant prompted them to say hello back to me and to smile.

And both these kids did exactly the same thing. They said hello all right, but for the smile their little mouths stretched open in a grimace that looked like it really hurt them. "This is a smile," they both said, and they held the "i" sound for a long time so that the word sounded like a form of torture.

It was awful, just because the expression on their faces, with all their teeth showing, had nothing to do with a real smile. This was some artificial thing they'd been taught to do so that they might fit better into the big wide stupid world.

And it strikes me as absolutely wrong to do this to them because this isn't who they are.

I want Timmy to grow — naturally — out of the person he already is. I don't want him subjected to "normalization techniques" that twist his soul out of shape.

Timmy's one of the reasons I don't cut my hair. When he was a baby he liked to grab on to it, and the strength of his tiny hands just amazed me. Even now when he gets really frightened he likes me to hug him with my hair loose so it kind of covers him.

I had a real scare with him a few nights ago though. Mom was out with Lancelot and I went to check on Timmy.

I really panicked when I saw his bed was empty. I couldn't find him anywhere in the house. I kept calling and calling, trying not to get too hysterical.

I made myself breathe deeply and calm down a bit. I sat on his bedroom floor and then I noticed his shoes were missing.

Next I high-tailed it outside with a flashlight. We live in an old rented farmhouse and it's pretty isolated and there is a long drive up to the road. And that's where I found him trudging up the drive with his swimming trunks in a plastic bag.

He had his trainers on, but he can't tie the laces yet, and that was great, because the trailing laces really slowed him down. I can't stand to think what might have happened if he had made it to the road.

"Where are you going, Timmy?" I asked him.

"Goin' swimmum, Juss," he said. (He can't say "Jess" very well yet.)

It took a bit of work to persuade him to go back to the house and to make him understand that the swimming pool would be closed and dark and that it's dangerous for him to go off on his own like that.

Timmy can be very, very stubborn, and if he wants to do something, he just ups and does it.

I think it's wonderful that he loves the swimming so much, but his escapade that night really frightened me.

APART

This is probably the longest letter I have written to anyone, and I hope you don't find it too boring.

I want to tell you something now I have never told anyone. Sometimes when Timmy gets in one of his really frantic, worked-up states, he scratches me on my arms really hard. I have to wear long-sleeved shirts all the time so that people don't see the marks.

But the thing is, I just let him do it. I let him dig his nails in and really hurt me. Because sometimes it seems like that pain is something I deserve, or that I need to have done to me.

Let's make a pact not to hurt ourselves like this any more. Because it seems to me that when you use the dog clippers on yourself when you're depressed, that's what you're doing. It just makes my stomach clench to think of you buzzing your scalp and scraping yourself nearly bald. So no more of this kind of stuff. Okay by you?

I really like the way you signed your last letter — "your prairie friend." It makes me feel connected in a real way to a part of the country I will probably never see. I try to picture all that endless space you have in your part of the world and it feels sort of like infinity.

I am happy to think of you moving through all that space in your calico car with Coyote contented beside you in the passenger seat. Even though Coyote probably doesn't enjoy second-hand smoke.

Take care of yourself.

With much affection,

Jessica

December 3

Dear Jess:

I'm sorry it's taken so long to answer your last letter, but as you can see, I have a new address. Your letter took a while to get here, having stopped at my folks' place first, judging by the NOT AT THIS ADDRESS scrawled across the envelope. My mother's writing. She knows perfectly well where I am.

I'm at Uncle Jerry's cabin.

Mail only comes here three days a week, and it's a thirty-minute hike to the Kroeker Lake post office. True, I can drive most of it, but The Beast complains mightily about the lousy road — which is actually better now that snow has fallen and filled some of the holes. I have a good fire going and hauled water in from a hole I chopped in the ice so I can relax now and tell you everything.

One of the few things Uncle Jerry salvaged from his former life as a dentist is this cabin. It's in one of the little subdivisions that surround Kroeker Lake (pronounced Kray-ker) and sits in a cluster of trees on the south shore of the lake itself. The dominant wind is from the north, so it collects all its strength, sweeps across the lake ice and drives the frost right through the walls. It's pretty though — blue-blowing snow in that eerie half-light we have at 5 p.m. I live in my coat, even though I've got electricity. I keep blowing breakers trying to avoid becoming an ice cube. The fire's roaring, but I think most of the heat's going straight up the chimney.

Notice I'm putting off telling you why I'm here.

I got kicked out of home. The reason I got kicked out of home was because I got kicked out of school — again. And this time it wasn't even my fault.

Well, maybe a bit.

It was The Beast. A combination of The Beast and my dad.

It got cold. The Beast wouldn't start four days in a row, and so I missed my first class all four days. If you "skip" four classes in a week, you get suspended for a day. That's the rule at Evelyn Weekes Comprehensive. No excuses. (Evelyn Weekes must be quite the old gal. They named a school after her, AND SHE'S STILL ALIVE! Scary.) Now, I don't care if I get suspended for a day. I don't care if I'm suspended for a WEEK. But my dad does. I was on "probation" according to him, "One more suspension and you're OUT, Smartass." So we had this big argument. If he'd have let me park in the garage, then my car would have started and I wouldn't have been late for anything. So it's his fault, right? Okay, maybe not but I blame him anyway.

Maybe making me park on the street was a plot to get me out of the house. If it was, it worked. My actual leaving was sort of interesting though. My mom disappeared somewhere. She was nowhere to be seen, but my weird little sister helped me pack the few things I took with me. She didn't do it in a I'm-glad-to-see-you-go way, but was actually trying to be helpful. It was a kind of surprise. Dad sat and read a newspaper. He gets two. It's a lot of work keeping up with the important news of the world and it gives him something to hide behind.

I admit I've been guilty of pretty well everything over the past couple of years. I admit to wearing a hat when I shouldn't have been wearing a hat (my freshly bald head was cold). I admit to giving Sheryl Sawanko the finger (she called me a dildo) and shooting mustard at Jennifer Greer (she shot ketchup at me). I admit to asking Mr. Enright what he did with his ruler besides point with it (he could have put out my eye, he was that close). I admit to bringing booze into school (once — it was an orange, shot with vodka). I admit to swinging David Charpentier by his heels from the school steps (he called my little sister "Sue LaDo" and he was NOT referring to her hair) and I admit to calling Mr. Roberts a "punctilious troglodyte asshole." (He is. He called me "supercilious" and "neoteric." Two can play the name-calling game.)

Anyway, coming late for four days and being kicked out of everything for it seems like overkill to me. The only one who sort of defended me was Hackles. He didn't actually say anything. He just sort of stood there staring at the floor with his lips all bunched together. Then he looked at me and unlocked his lips into a lob-sided smile and walked away. He was saying, "You gotta do what you gotta do."

The hell with the rest — and the carpet they rode in on. I'm fine. No one's going to bug me here. I cashed a thousand

APART

dollar bond my grandma gave me. It's from an account she set up for me a long time ago and neglected to lock me out. I knew it was for a rainy day and God, is it pouring now. Aside from raiding five hundred bucks from it for The Beast (for which I do feel somewhat guilty, but only because it's been such a lousy investment) I've saved it for just this sort of emergency.

It's not going to last forever though.

Nothing lasts forever, not even this cold, right?

I must tell you about Coyote.

I saw him on the way home today. Not too far from here. He crossed the road, stepped a few paces into the woods, then stopped, turned and watched me. Coyotes NEVER do that here. He was beautiful, too — a thick, rich coat, blue-flecked white with a roan belly. When I saw him in town I didn't get that good a look because the light wasn't good enough. Anyway, I swear it's the same one and that he's followed me here.

"Not bloody likely," I hear you say. (In my mind's ear you have an accent and as a Maritimer you probably do, but of course I don't have an accent at all — ha, ha — or what I have is as flat as a cow pie.) Okay, so you're right. How would he travel 300 km north from there? But he sure looks the same, and the way he looks at me. It's as though he's waiting for me to do something. The question is, what?

You used the word ecstasy to describe that feeling when you meet a creature eye to eye, and I guess it's something like that, but it's also scary and weird.

For instance, a small stream that feeds the lake (where I get my water) enters at a bay near Uncle Jerry's. A raft is anchored in the bay, frozen now into the ice. In summer it's a diving platform where I spent many happy hours when I was eleven or twelve, back when my parents were still talking to Uncle Jerry. You could lie on it and listen to the lapping water and watch the clouds race by. It floated outside time. And now it sits locked in ice. Someone forgot to pull it ashore for the winter.

But that's not what I want to tell you. I want to tell you about Coyote. I saw him this very morning standing on the raft. He looked as though he had just risen from his haunches. He cast a glance my way, then trotted ashore and disappeared into the low tangle of young spruce.

I imagine him lying on the raft, dreaming.

What do coyotes dream?

What do bears dream?

They do not dream of Gunner and his get-a-job-make-lots-of-money ways. They do not dream of Mr. Roberts the Troglodyte, or my dad the Frankenplant maker. They do dream though. Science has proven that. They twitch. They moan. They have REM.

They probably dream of eating or hunting. Or maybe of being hunted.

I've got a good fire going. The wind has calmed, and the northern lights are splashing above. I myself shall dream now. ("Shall" — I'm waxing poetic, eh?) What shall I dream? Maybe of you. What do you dream?

• • •

Another day, another dollar — except there is no dollar. And really, not much of a day either. There's a steady fog of frost lifting off the lake and landing right inside my bones. I swear it's warmer outside. I'm running out of fuel. I'm going to have to go into the woods and start chopping. The exercise will be good for me. It'll keep me warm. This afternoon.

Notice I'm writing little short choppy sentences? It's the equivalent of stomping my feet. Stomping my brain. To keep the blood flowing there. No, this is not nuts. It's a perfectly normal way of staying alive. And no, I don't think you're nuts either, and if in fact you are, I wish everyone was just as nuts as you.

I loved your retelling of Glooskap, the farting coyote trickster. Here the Cree call him Weysakechak. It's amazing those two names refer to the same thing. One would have to be informed to know.

Speaking of being informed, I should inform you of another reason Uncle Jerry is on the outs with my mom and dad. He's going with a woman who was born near here, as were the rest of her relatives for about 10,000 years. She is the sister to a guy he became friends with in prison. Her name is Elaine. She has ink black eyes and that same smile Coyote gave me the other day. She's the one who told me about Weysakechak.

I like her quite a lot. My parents though, do not. They could probably forgive Uncle Jerry for dealing prescription drugs, but they could never forgive him for going out with an "Indian."

I hope the two of them come out here soon (and bring some dry wood!) so I can tell her about your bear spirit sitting on the can reading philosophy. Elaine'll like that.

Your mom can't be all bad if she does cartwheels once a year to celebrate her birthday. I take it that you mean these are joyful cartwheels, not the kind my mom does as a sort of dexterity demo. She probably does acrobatics in bed for my dad. I can just see them — he's doing nothing — she's doing everything. Of course, she probably has to. I doubt he can get it up.

Most people refuse to think about their parents' sex life. Mine are so obvious about it, what with the beige leather and Harley, it's sick. Beige sex. That's funny.

On top of their weird sexual stuff, Dad does his Frankenplants gig. I agree all those seeds should be flushed down the toilet, except you know what would happen then — they'd grow all over the place.

I wish my dad could see the light. But no, he's like some kind of comic book evil scientist — except he's for real. He's so smart. God, I hope I don't grow up to be like that. The armchair psychologist sitting on my left brain is saying, "Yes, and that's probably why you got yourself kicked out of school."

Probably.

You pay a price trying to get what you don't want.

And THAT sounds like a bad line in a country and western song.

And so does Lancelot (Lance a lot?) Beauchemin (Pretty road?). A mechanic, eh? A knight in shining coveralls. Maybe just what your mom needs. Safe, reliable…pot-bellied. Safe and reliable = pot-bellied, right? Maybe she'll stop sobbing herself to sleep at night over Gunner. Maybe Gunner will show up on your door step with a handful of flowers.

Maybe she's not crying for Gunner at all.

You don't. Why do you assume she does?

Of all the things I know about you, and really, I don't know much, I admire your devotion to your little brother. Is it despite his handicap, or because of it? I ask because as I was leaving the house, I saw my little sister Sue as a human being for the first time in my life. A person in her own right. I was surprised and a little bit sad to leave her alone with those people — our parents.

She stood there at the door and raised her hand. She stood motionless, without expression on her face. Perhaps she had no face to go with goodbye. She didn't know how to make it — like Timmy's classmates made a smile that goes with hello.

I must have a bit of Tim in me — in the stubborn department. Except no one trudged up the lane to get me when I left home to go to the swimming pool — you know, when I got in The Beast and drove north.

I'm here. And it's dark. And it's cold.

Do you want to know something?

Timmy doesn't know he's hurting you. Only you know. The only pact we can make is not to hurt each other.

I can promise you that. Can you?

Love,

Your woodsy friend, Sween

December 12

Dear Sween:

Your letter stirred so many strong feelings in me, I hardly know where to begin. So I'm going to try to unravel my reactions the same way I unbraid my hair, a strand at a time.

First off, I really hope that when you read this letter you are snug and warm, and that your uncle and Elaine have arrived. Does your Uncle Jerry have room for you to stay with him in the city? Is that a possibility?

I hate the idea of your being cold and uncomfortable and hungry in your isolated cabin. What food supplies do you have there, Sween? Have you got any fruit or greens?

I wish with all my heart that I were rich and that I could send you lots of money.

I guess I am still shocked by what happened to you. I am shocked and so angry at your parents, I would like to fly through the air like a hate-filled djinn and shake them until their perfect (no doubt very white) teeth rattle in their pointy heads.

Because you're right. You did absolutely nothing to justify getting kicked out. The way you've been treated is colos-

APART

sally unfair. I wish I could help you in some practical way. But apart from letters and good positive thoughts, I can't think of how to do that.

Thank goodness for Coyote. And of course I believe he is the same one you saw in the city.

It makes me feel so much better that he is with you. This is one smart coyote, Sween. But then he would be. He chose you because he knows how super extraordinarily exceptional you are.

I really respect you for heading out to the bush on your own. I respect your courage and the fact that you are able to be alone. Not everybody can do that. A lot of people are afraid to be by themselves. That's why people like Gunner and all his buddies always have to have the television going or the radio cranked up. They create a kind of fortress of noise around themselves and they don't see that the noise is making them numb to who they are.

I know how scary and strange it is when you meet your spirit animal eye to eye. It is frightening, even when I meet my bear in dreams. A good fear, though, that shakes me up and says, "Wake up, Jessica, and look at the world."

I hope you figure out soon what it is you have to do, Sween — whatever move you think Coyote is waiting for you to make.

You said the only pact we can make is not to hurt each other. I've been thinking about that a lot, and what a huge promise this is.

Of course I want to make that promise to you. Your letters

have touched my mind and soul in a way no person on earth ever has before. I want desperately to make that promise to you, and to keep it. But I look around and it seems to me that people are always hurting each other without meaning to. It's almost as if being human and gobbling up space and air in this world means you are going to hurt other creatures. Maybe unconsciously, but we hurt them just the same.

I mean, I love Great-Grandma Doig with all my heart. She believes in me and my abilities. She gives me great books to read and encourages me in my dream of becoming a writer. She genuinely loves Timmy. But she sometimes says things that really upset me. Things that make me really disappointed in her.

I am sure she doesn't mean to be unkind. It is just that she has some ideas I think are really wrong-headed. I could say bigoted, but she is an old lady and I love her, and that word seems way too harsh. Maybe she's prejudiced or narrow-minded or intolerant. These words all seem wrong too, because she is so filled with love. But...

For example, sometimes she goes on about how new immigrants are taking over the country by having so many babies, and that soon there will be no white people left.

This would make me laugh if it didn't also make me want to cry. I mean, it's out and out racist. I know I shouldn't idealize Great-Grandma Doig, but I do. And then when she comes out with one of these really dumb comments, I feel hurt and let down. And then she'll go and show off the pictures of the African children she's sponsored in the Save the

Children fund, using a good portion of her pension to do so. It makes your head swim.

Have you ever heard of the Jains? They are a religious group in India and they wear gauze over their faces so that they don't breathe in or swallow any tiny insects by mistake. (Which actually would not be a bad idea around here in June for the black flies.) The Jains always carry a tiny brush with them, and they sweep the path in front of them gently as they walk so that they don't step on anything living and tiny and fragile.

If that sounds like a weird over-bothersome way to live, then maybe it shows just how difficult and complex the promise not to hurt someone else really is.

And you're thinking, "Oh no, Jess has been dipping into the spirit bear's philosophy books again."

Maybe I am just trying to keep my mind off the idea of you reading this letter in the cold and the dark.

I do not like to think of you in the cold and dark, Sween.

If you think of a way I can help you, let me know, please.

I hope your father's Harley falls to bits over the winter. Or that he forgets to drain the oil and the pistons all seize. I hope armies of stinging ants invade your parents' beige leathers.

These are not Jain-like thoughts, but I don't care.

I think of your little sister helping you pack, and how she had no expression to go with saying goodbye. And that thought makes me extremely sad for both of you.

Will you write to her, Sween?

I am glad you have seen who your sister really is, even

though it took such a painful situation to bring that revelation about.

I had to think long and hard about your question about what you call my "devotion" to Timmy. I suppose I think of it simply as love.

Is it despite his handicap, or because of it? That was your question.

And here's the answer.

I love him because he is Timmy; because he is absolutely himself. He is direct. He is honest. He is guileless. (I mean he is never deceitful or conniving or manipulative in any way — but isn't that a great word?)

I love him because he will suddenly tug at my hand and say, "Look, Juss," and his face is full of wonder. He will point to the sky and I will see a bird through his eyes as the purest, most exalted thing ever created.

I love him because he trusts me and he comes to me when he is afraid.

I love him for his stubbornness.

I love him because he can make me laugh, especially when he creates his own metaphors — like "Put that Gunner in the garbage." (He really did come up with that one on his own.)

I love him because in the times I have felt darkest, he has been my whole reason for living.

Timmy gives me far more than I have ever given him. He has taught me to look at things in a totally fresh way. I mean really look, so that you get kind of immersed in and excited about what you are seeing.

APART

Although Timmy can also see things I will never be able to see. He'll point to the corner of his bedroom and laugh. Then I look where he's pointing, but there's nothing there.

What do you think he sees that makes him so happy? Maybe he sees joyful children who lived and played in this old farmhouse many years ago. Or maybe he sees the memories of adults who are thinking of their childhood here at that very moment. Or maybe he sees Coyote dancing on a hilltop with a big orange moon behind him.

Timmy can see the future. There have been lots of times that he told me things would happen, and then they did.

Lately he's been saying something I hope he's wrong about.

I had to stop there because unfortunately, the thing Timmy predicted came true. Over the past couple of weeks he's told me every day, "Gunner's cumin, Juss. Gunner's cumin." And he didn't sound very happy about this, believe me.

Every time he said it my heart sank. But I kept telling myself maybe Timmy had it wrong.

He didn't.

Late yesterday afternoon, a royal blue Rolls-Royce came sailing down the snowy laneway. I thought it was Lancelot who had rented or borrowed it as part of a surprise special date for Mom.

The car glided to a stop in front of the house and out stepped my pretty-boy father in an expensive-looking suit that fitted him like a glove. I had never seen him in a suit before, and I have to admit he looked amazing.

Then I felt sick. I realized I had got what I wanted when I paid for that ad in the *Globe and Mail* back in July. My father had come home. Except now I had come to the conclusion that Mom was better off without him.

And I thought, here's one of those ironies that Shakespeare was so fond of. You feel the twist of fate stick the knife in, and you taste the bitterness on your tongue.

And you want to spit.

You've got what you wanted, except that now it's a curse.

Your letter said, "Maybe Gunner will show up with a handful of flowers."

Well, he didn't have flowers, but he did have a lot of Christmas presents, all beautifully wrapped in paper so bright and pretty that Timmy kept stroking it.

The big question at the back of my mind was, where did Gunner get the money for all this?

The answer to that had to wait a while because Mom just about bowled me over, running to leap into his arms. I swear I could feel the heat radiating from her as she passed me. She was positively glowing with happiness, and that is no cliché. Her cheeks were rosy. Her eyes were bright. She looked as if she could actually have flown through the air if she'd wanted to.

That's my dilemma. She adores him. Being with Archibald (dread forbidden word) William Doig makes my mom happier than anything else on earth. Even though he is a complete asshole. (Pardon my vulgarity, but that is putting it mildly in any case.)

They went straight to Mom's bedroom and shut the door.

APART

I put my fingers in my ears, and then I put on one of the records Timmy loves best. (Yes, we still have a record player. There are kids at school who look at me bug-eyed when I tell them that. I don't tell them about the disconnected dial phone.)

I bet you won't believe me when I tell you that this record Timmy likes so much is excerpts from the opera *Carmen*. He just loves this music, especially the children's marching chorus near the beginning.

He always does the same thing when the music starts. He holds the album cover out at arm's length, and he stares at the picture of Carmen with her red dress and her cigarette. He keeps looking at the album cover as he whirls round and round in a circle. He can whirl that way for ten minutes straight and he never gets dizzy, maybe because he's keeping his eyes fixed on that one object.

Anyway, between the *Carmen* arias and Timmy's twirling, I was able to block out most of the noises coming from the bedroom.

Maybe none of us likes thinking of our parents "doing the dirty" (one of the ways Gunner likes to describe sex, and I kid you not) let alone having to hear them. I know you joke about your parents' beige sex, but it's just too personal a thing to have to listen to anybody doing. Or that's just how it strikes me. Maybe I am a tightass like Gunner says. (And I know I'll be hearing a lot of that phrase again now that he's back with us — for a while anyway.)

Maybe sex makes me uncomfortable because it's so much in our faces all the time, and because of the way it's presented with people in way-too-tight clothes and a lot of cheap vulgar jokes. I don't see much of the kind of sexual love I imagine has to exist somewhere with kindness and caring and a gentle touch at the heart of it. I'm not seeing that anywhere at all really.

I am really sorry to be inflicting you with what is probably my super extraordinarily wacky hang-up, Sween, particularly when you are in such a difficult situation right now. A cold situation.

As I said, I hope you are warm when you read this and that Uncle Jerry and Elaine are there too.

Anyway, after Mom and Gunner finally emerged from the bedroom, I found out where the Rolls and presents came from. The answer is Mrs. Oliphant. She's a very rich widow who lives in a big house in Fredericton, and she is apparently deluded enough to be employing The Gunner as her chauffeur and general handyman. Which explains the suit. It's actually a uniform.

If she let him borrow the Rolls and gave him money to buy presents for his wife and children, it sounds like she is another in the endless line of women who get besotted by him. Who knows what happened to Gloria? I bet Mom isn't asking because her primary goal in life is to keep the almighty Gunner happy.

How often have I heard "Now don't say anything to upset your father"?

Well, I don't have to open my mouth at all. The Gunner just has to look at me to get worked up. "Still the same old sourpuss, eh, Jessica? Your looks certainly haven't improved since I've been away, girl."

Timmy's taken to wearing his earmuffs in the house since Gunner got back. I think there's more to it than trying to shut out The Gunner's voice and his noisy old rock 'n' roll (my father thinks wrinkled, creepy Mick Jagger sits next to God). I think he wants to shut out Gunner altogether.

"Put that Gunner in the garbage." Timmy's got one of those clear voices that carry a long way. And he doesn't realize that his voice gets louder when he has his earmuffs on.

I was trying to hush him up, saying shush and putting my finger to my lip. Gunner always maintains he can't understand a word Timmy says, but I was really afraid he might get the gist this time.

"Christ!" Gunner exploded. "Isn't that kid weird enough without wearing earmuffs in the house to top it off? People will think we live in a goddamn loony bin."

I felt all the hair at the back of my neck prickle because Gunner in a rage is always a super scary situation.

"He's nothing but a goddamn embarrassment," Gunner started screaming. "What are my friends going to think?"

This seemed like a really stupid question to me as The Gunner's friends have names like Snake Eyes and Snorter and Captain Chaos. Their idea of a great social skill is downing a bottle of beer in one swallow.

"Get those goddamn things off his head!" Gunner made a grab for the earmuffs and Timmy ducked and went into a fetal crouch right there beside the table.

{77}

I felt sick.

Then Gunner tried to grab the earmuffs again but Timmy was ready for him. He bit Gunner on the hand, pretty hard.

I felt sicker. But I was ready too.

I got in between Timmy and my father so that when The Gunner's hand came down in a wallop, he hit me instead.

Then something weird happened to me, even though I profess to non-violence and admire the Jains so much.

I head-butted The Gunner in his rock-hard belly. Maybe I was inspired by Carmen and the bulls and the matadors. Anyway, Gunner went down on his ass.

For a split second I felt jubilant. But not for long. Because The Gunner was up on his feet, and he took one swing at me that laid me flat.

It's a really frightening thing to discover just how much physically stronger your father is than you, especially when you hate each other's guts.

Mom started trying to cool things out, and then she drove me and Timmy to Great-Grandma Doig's. With us out of the way, Mom could devote herself to calming and soothing her "sweetie pie." (Every time I hear her call him that, I want to put on Timmy's earmuffs myself.)

Of course, I am the one who is in the wrong because I shouldn't have "crossed my father."

I should just have stood there and let him whop Timmy around the head.

No way, José.

APART

I can't tell you how much I hate him. It can't be healthy to hate someone this much.

Great-Grandma Doig says that Gunner was spoiled rotten as a child ("I loved my daughter-in-law dearly, but she did everything for that child but breathe") so he never really grew up.

That's why Timmy and I are stuck with an immature, self-obsessed kid for a father.

You're right, Sween. We have to pay a high price in order not to be like our parents.

I'm thinking of my spirit bear really hard these days, and of that wonderful light we're speeding toward with the cold air on his fur and my skin. Maybe we're coming on the north wind that's heading across the lake for your cabin, Sween. Maybe the bear is taking the bite out of it, so that it becomes a blessed wind.

This comes with my love, Sween.

Your true friend in N.B.,

Jessica

Dear Jessica:

So much has happened since we last spoke — not the least of it to YOU. (What's Gunner up to? Something, that's for sure.) I hardly know where to begin. We're repeating each other's opening phrases about not knowing where to begin. I think what it really means is that this letter writing is great but is missing the spontaneity of real live conversation with someone face to face. But never mind, it might just be me starving for company.

Speaking of starving, I can answer one of your questions straight off. It's amazing what you can do with a can opener and a bag of rice. I have both, so I'm in good shape. You can get quite creative blending beans with ravioli, say, or chunky stew on rice. Okay, I'm missing big time on my fresh veggies, but I bought a bag of lemons that I mistook for oranges. They were kind of yellow, you know, like underdone but I thought they would last longer because they had more time to ripen. Idiot. Now everything has lemon in it. Then I found some ginger, and lemon with ginger in it is pretty good too.

The mail is somewhat slower here than in the rest of the

world. I think I mentioned that it only comes three times a week. I also think they still deliver it by runner and dog sled. So what with all the holidays, terrorist bombs and general incompetence, your letter did not arrive till after Christmas. I don't mind saying that I could have used it BEFORE.

It's pretty dismal out here when it's really cold and there's a wind. I have to go out and chop enough wood to keep me going for the day. Occasionally, I chop enough for two. That usually takes care of my mornings. I have a radio and a TV. The radio comes in pretty much filled with static and the TV gets one snowy (CBC) station. When I get tired of listening to the static and watching the snow on TV, I turn everything off and listen to the wind and watch the snow out the window. Nothing much changes.

After I've stoked the fire, I hike over to the Stone's Throw Restaurant (Garage, Confectionery, Post Office, Liquor Board Store and Gas Bar), sit in a window booth and have a coffee (three milks, four sugars — two refills). I take out my notebook and sometimes write. It's actually more of a prop, since I don't generally get much down on paper. But it looks good. It's where I write this letter to you.

Gladys is the woman who works here all the time. She runs the Post Office and the Restaurant. You've got to understand that this restaurant consists of a short counter with three stools at it, and three booths along the front window. Sometimes there are a couple of guys in skidoo suits sitting at the counter flirting with Gladys.

She'd be my mother's age and she likes to tease me. She

calls me The Writer. "Oh, and how's The Writer today?" "Whatcha writin' about today? You writin' about me?" "I bet you're writin' that girl in Nova Scotia." I don't correct her re your whereabouts. "Hey, watch what you're saying or he'll put it in his book," she'll say if there's someone there. I like her though. You can tell she's had a hard life. Her eyes look like they've seen through a lot of dark time, and she's jumpy and jerky, like maybe she's done a lot of drugs or something. Maybe she's just really nervous. But she's nice to me. I try to be nice back.

Anyway, she's about the only human being I talk to here.

A few days before Christmas she says, "Did they find you?"

I said, "Who?"

She said, "Whoever was looking for you."

She described the car (silver Volvo) and I guess my dad was too lazy or paranoid or whatever to walk the five minutes from the road to the cabin.

Anyway, they didn't send in the RCMP to find me, so I know nothing major has happened, like someone dying.

It also made me homesick. So I went back. Just for a visit.

That saying about you can't go home anymore? True.

My parents invited me in for supper. It was like I was a stranger. They made small talk. Some corporation or other matched Dad's half mil bumping it up to a full million. That was pretty much all he babbled about. My mom smiled and nodded at everything he said. My sister came down from her room, never made eye contact and never said a word more than pass the water, then excused herself the moment we were done and disappeared again.

The only one who seemed excited to see me was Zamboni. But he's growing some kind of goiter on his neck (this in a month!) and although I would have liked to take him with me, I doubt he's much longer for this world. And if he is, I couldn't afford the vet bills.

I tried calling a couple friends but nobody was in. I went to a movie that was playing at the university (cheap). It was *The Deer Hunter*. Ever seen it? Don't. I was expecting something Christmassy but it was about this guy looking for another guy from the army, and finds him in Vietnam (I think) where he's a drug addict making a living playing Russian roulette — two guys sit in a ring, one bullet. It's a competitive sporting event that people bet on. He keeps surviving. He's valuable as this commodity whose odds keep getting tighter. He's going to get it sooner than later. But he keeps doing it. Meanwhile, his buddy keeps looking for him. Is he going to kill himself before his friend finds him? I got a depression on top of my depression.

Still, that wasn't the worst of it. I climbed back in The Beast and pointed it north again. About two hours later, not far from the cabin, two silver eyes reflected back to me from the middle of the snow-covered road.

I tried to stop, but I hit it.

I stopped and turned around so I could shine my lights on whatever it was. As I got closer I could see a small figure dragging itself in the ditch.

It was Coyote.

He was dragging himself backwards toward the woods. I'd broken his front legs. He was whimpering. I wanted to catch him, take him home and heal him. I ran through the snow. I kept stumbling, the drifts were so deep. But he disappeared into the black woods before I got to him.

The next day, as soon as it got light enough, I went back to see if I could find him. I couldn't. I couldn't even find the place where I'd hit him. I was left with the eerie impossible feeling that maybe it hadn't happened. Maybe I'd dreamt it. But I know it had.

There was a tuft of fur stuck in the bumper of my car.

That was my Christmas day.

Hope yours was better.

On Boxing Day Uncle Jerry and Elaine showed up. Which was a good thing because I was still in bed inside my sleeping bag. I didn't care if I ever got out of that bag again. Maybe if I died I would meet Coyote's spirit someplace and I could apologize to him properly. Maybe make it up to him somehow.

Elaine brought a ton of food and showed me how to make bannock. You've never tasted anything so good when it's hot with butter dripping off it and smothered in strawberry jam.

Uncle Jerry showed me where the auger was and how to use it (I'd been thawing snow for water after the stream and lake ice got too thick to break through). He'd also brought a truck (and trailer) load of wood, which I thought we'd have

APART

to lug from the road. But he just drove out onto the lake and around to the front door. We piled the wood right up against the cabin. He was pleased with the way I'd been cleaning out all the windfalls around the place. He also showed me the tricks of starting his ancient chainsaw (I'd been using a buck saw till then because I couldn't keep his chainsaw running).

They stayed a couple of days till New Year's Eve. I was glad they came. Elaine said Coyote had probably wanted to go to the Great Spirit and I had helped send him there. So he would have been grateful and that I could still count on his spirit.

I don't believe much in that kind of stuff. But I hope she's right.

I spent New Year's Eve at the Stone's Throw. Gladys had a party. Everybody got drunk — except me. I was the taxi.

So now it's the new year and I know I'm not going to last much longer here. I'm trying to decide what to do. I don't want to go back to the city, with Uncle Jerry or anybody else. I always fall into the same routines and end up in the same places and the same state of mind. The same circles go round and round.

My parents are just who they are. There's nothing you or I or anybody else can do about it. It's pretty clear that I can never go home again. I don't feel like going to school right now either, although I'm sure I will go back eventually. Just not now.

I know what you mean about being human means hurting other creatures, whether intentional or not. My little sister hurt me a lot with her silence. I thought some little bridge had been crossed the day I left — but I was either very wrong or she turned around and went back across it leaving me alone on the other side. And then there's what I did to Coyote.

I just don't ever want to do anything to hurt you. If I do, you must tell me. I know you would never try to hurt me either, but in that way the world is an accident, you might by accidental chance obliterate me — as I might you. But never intentionally. It's the best we can do — without carrying it to the extreme extent of the Jains and their gauze masks. (Wherever did you hear about that? You are FULL of the most weird bits of knowledge.)

I hope you're not planning on heading into a nunnery. When I hear that word, I always think of "winery" — they sound sort of the same. You go in a fresh young grape and come out corked in a bottle.

I'm sorry you have such reservations about sex but if it wasn't so much fun, it wouldn't have been around for such a long time. I don't have anything against it, at least the idea of it. I have to admit I don't have a lot of practical experience. Except for what I got with Maryanne Ravenhurst, the blonde ten-of-ten of grade ten. I was in total lust. (Thank God she moved away in grade eleven. I might be a daddy now, bouncing baby Sweens on my knees.) But I understand what you mean by how it's so exploited — especially to sell things. Harley ads always have women draped over them, naked except for some leather thongs (not beige).

I do admire you taking on Gunner — both you and Get-Him-in-the-Garbage Tim. I would never have thought about head-butting though, at least not in the stomach. Now if you'd got his nose, the gushing blood would have slowed him down. So remember that for next time (with full apologies to the Jains). There are other equally vulnerable body parts, notably one that is lower than his six-pack belly. Shakespeare would approve. So would Bear.

Your father may be immature and self-obsessed but at least you know where you stand with him. I have no idea why mine came looking for me — if that was him. The subject never came up over dinner, and he's not the kind of guy you ask a direct question.

What if I wanted to send you an urgent message? How would I do it? Courier I guess, if a courier would go to such a place as New Brunswick.

Gladys tells me the mail man is coming soon to pick up (and drop off) the mail here. I'll say goodbye for now.

As always,

Sween

Dear Sween:

I really hope this letter reaches you quickly. I felt like a horse had kicked me in the stomach when I read your description of Coyote's accident. I can imagine very well how wretched this made you feel.

But I am sure Elaine is absolutely right, and that Coyote's spirit is still with you. At least we can hope.

I've been thinking that perhaps the accident was a kind of hallucination brought on by the movie you saw. *The Deer Hunter* sounds dangerously depressing. I would probably want to pull the covers over my head for a week if I watched a film like that. I think I've told you how really down I can get if I watch movies where people are being gunned down or run down, and everyone is sick and cruel and sad, sad, sad.

That goes for what I read as well. I have to be really careful because my thoughts can get easily infected. You know how Hamlet says, "There's nothing either good or bad, but thinking makes it so." Well, I do know, from lots of personal experience, that it's dangerous to let your thoughts get polluted by the one-sided ugly views of the world. It sounds as if

The Deer Hunter is one of those major pollutants. Maybe it infected your thoughts, so that you thought you had hit Coyote, but in fact you hadn't.

Or maybe Coyote staged the whole thing, and he's tricking you for some reason. Coyote and my bear are way smarter and super extraordinarily more subtle than we are.

I am glad you have Gladys in the coffee shop to talk to, and when you described how your Uncle Jerry and Elaine showed up on Boxing Day, I just about cheered. Bannock and an auger and water and wood and good company. They brought you wonderful gifts and these are what you deserve.

You seem to be undergoing a lot of trials right now, Sween, above and beyond the hardships you took on by going to the cabin on your own. It's like the stories of heroes who have to undergo test after test to prove they are fit for their destiny.

I wish there were a way I could help you more, and you are right that letters can't be as spontaneous as a face-to-face conversation. But they are what we have. They are the rope that links us, and I believe it's a real rope we can cling on to when either of us thinks we're going under.

It never occurred to me before that I am lucky in my relationship with Gunner simply because I know exactly where we stand. I despise him, and he despises me. I can't see that ever changing. It amazes me when I hear girls at school talk about their fathers with real warmth and affection. I know I will never experience a father's love, and I wonder what it would feel like.

I wonder, most of all, how I might be a different person if

I had a father who loved me and who told me I was talented and attractive. A father who made me feel special.

If selling or dumping your children was legal, I am quite sure Gunner would have got rid of me and Timmy by now. I've heard him talking to Mom sometimes when he is drunk. He keeps saying that Timmy and I can't possibly be his. He is so cruel it makes me sick.

I know he would like to have a really pretty daughter, blonde and sweet-faced and delicate like my mom. He'd like a son whom he could teach to take engines apart and then reassemble them; a son he could watch play hockey and football.

Your father is obviously a lot smarter than mine. And that makes it much harder for you to know what he's thinking and what his motives are. I don't get it either. Why would he drive so far to find you and then not actually look for Uncle Jerry's cabin? Why would he be so indifferent when you showed up for Christmas dinner?

How can your mother just let you go off like that without asking if you are cold in the cabin or if you need anything? Your little sister is probably scared and brainwashed by the rules of life in Shaunavon Heights. She needs a lot of understanding. You and I both know just how much willpower and courage it takes to withstand our parents' ideas and demands and not become just like them.

Our Christmas Day was pretty subdued compared with the confrontation Gunner and I had the day he came home. Mom took me aside and made me promise not to talk back to Gunner or "upset" him. She must have spoken to Gunner as

APART

well, because he essentially ignored me and Timmy except to give us our gifts.

I wondered if Mrs. Oliphant had chosen them. I got a pink cashmere sweater — very lovely and soft. But pink does not look good on me. When I put it on, Gunner smirked and turned his face away. Enough said.

Timmy's present was an electronic gizmo with a screen on it. You're supposed to play games with it, but he isn't interested in it at all. He just picked it up and put it down again right away.

I feel so selfish rattling on about my home life when your situation is so much worse. It's as if you are already an adult and I'm still a kid clinging to her family.

At any rate, Great-Grandma gave me a poetry anthology that is packed full of treasures. When we actually get to meet some day, I'll show you the ones I like best. And maybe you can show me what you've been working at yourself.

Gladys calls you The Writer because she sees what your destiny is. And maybe this is the reason for all your trials now. Maybe this is the "dark night of the soul" every good writer has to go through in order to be perceptive and empathetic and honest. Or maybe you think I am being a super extraordinary romantic fool for thinking this way?

I had to stop there because our furnace conked out, and Timmy and I were walking around with extra socks on, and wrapped in blankets.

The furnace repair man came pretty quickly, which is

great because it is going to 50 below tonight with the wind chill. I have never known it to be so cold for so long here. They have cancelled the school buses, and Timmy and I are on our own for a few days because Mom has gone to stay with Gunner at Mrs. Oliphant's. Apparently he has his own apartment right inside her mansion.

This sounds to me like something out of the movies, or a bad novel. We heard an awful lot about Mrs. Oliphant's wealth and her "exquisite taste" in the few days Gunner was here.

Mrs. Oliphant really wanted to meet Mom, he said. I wonder what is going on here too, Sween. What is Gunner up to?

I know him. He is not going to be happy being a chauffeur for long, no matter how classy the car is. And of course I wonder if Mrs. Oliphant has fallen for my dear father. Maybe she wants to meet Mom to size up the competition.

Whenever Gunner said Mrs. Oliphant's name, which was pretty often, Timmy started chanting "elefunt, elefunt," and gallomping around with his arms swinging together in front of him. I thought his elephant imitation was pretty funny, but The Gunner was not amused.

"Shut that kid up," he said. "Show some respect."

I am sure Mrs. Oliphant has heard a lot of references to elephants in her time, and I couldn't see how Timmy was being disrespectful. But the long and the short of it was that Timmy and I spent a lot of the Christmas vacation in his room.

So my parents got to cuddle and kiss and lie about in bed

together as much as they wanted. Mom looked radiant and that's a fact.

Maybe I have let the Gunner's smutty jokes and all his boasting about "doing the dirty" ruin the idea of sexual love for me. Maybe my views will change once I get away from my parents altogether. Maybe my real problem is that I want too much — some kind of sublime transport together with another person, and not just something physical that happens in a bed or the back seat of a car.

In any case, there are far more pressing matters that need to be looked after right now, like keeping Timmy warm and making sure he doesn't wander outside when it's 50 below. He doesn't feel the cold the way you and I would. It's got something to do with his nerve endings not being as close to the skin as most people's are.

And that can be dangerous, because although he doesn't feel the cold, he is just as vulnerable to frostbite and skin damage as anyone else. Last week I caught him trying to go outside with his bare feet in the snow!

I've also got a problem with Lancelot. Remember him? Well, he has been making some really abusive phone calls for a few days now. (Now that Gunner has a salary and Mom is working, the phone is hooked up again. A very mixed blessing.) He yells in the phone — I think he must be really drunk — calling Mom all kinds of nasty names in both official languages.

Last night was a particularly bad one. He called nine times.

I don't say anything to him. I just hang up quietly once he starts going on.

He just called again now, and this time I thought he said in French that he was going to burn our house down. This really gives me the creeps, let me tell you.

I am writing to you now as I watch out the front window. I think I told you we have a really long drive down to the road, so I can see car headlights coming toward the house from a long way off.

I had to break off writing again, because all of a sudden I saw the headlights of a small truck turn off the road and start up our drive. It was too dark for me to make out whether it was Lancelot's, but in any case, he has access to lots of different vehicles because of managing the car lot.

I was sitting with the phone ready to call 9-1-1, and I had Timmy all dressed in his coat and boots and hat and scarf in case we had to make a run for it.

Then a really odd and wonderful thing happened. The truck stopped halfway down our drive, and I saw a shadowy shape cross in front of it. Next I heard a high-pitched squeal (it might have been an owl's cry). My heart was thumping hard.

Then the truck reversed really fast and took off down the road.

It's a real cliché, isn't it, to say I have never been so scared in all my life? But it's true.

I guess it was Lancelot. Who else could it have been?

But the crazy thing is that when I went outside, I saw a couple of big paw prints on the snow on our front porch, as though a large dog had been sitting there. And there was a drop of blood between the prints.

This is all true, Sween, I swear.

Maybe Coyote is still around and heading east.

Timmy and I are both fine, so don't worry about us at all.

You asked how you could get in touch urgently if you needed to. Our number here is (506) 563-7285. For as long as it lasts this time.

This comes with lots of love from me and Timmy. We hope you are warm and well and not watching any depressing films on TV.

Your true friend in N.B.,

Jessica

February 2

Dear Jess:

You can tell by how this is put together that I've been assembling this letter over a day or two. I suppose it's only been the usual two or three weeks, but when you're waiting it seems longer. I want to write this short section here and then hit the road. I didn't want to leave without hearing from you first, as though I would get in some kind of trouble by writing you out of turn.

I'm heading east. My ultimate destination is Matagouche, but I really don't know. I may be assuming a lot. For instance that The Beast will even make it that far, that I won't get abducted by aliens or Hells Angels (but they don't go out in winter, right?), but most important, that I'll be welcome by the only person I know who lives in that area of the world. One thing's for sure, I don't have enough money. Four new tires, plus a starter motor, a battery and a sleeping bag, plus various living expenses have pretty well depleted my cash. So, I'm going to have to work here and there along the way — shovel snow, wash dishes — whatever, I don't care.

So here's my plan. If you can make three copies of your

letters (okay, two copies plus the original), send them to the General Delivery in Kenora, Kapuskasing and Pembroke. Care of me, of course.

I don't know how long it's going to take me to get to those places but they are along the route I plan to take. I'm assuming I'll get through Manitoba without too much problem, but after that I don't know. I also don't know any French, so there's no point in having you send things to Quebec, even though I might end up there. But according to the map, it's close enough to hitchhike — at least it doesn't look far, an inch or so. Ha, ha.

At any rate, I'm thinking ol' Coyote is giving me some kind of vision that I don't normally have, as you'll read about in my "pre-written" part of the letter that's enclosed.

I do want to respond before I go about why my dad came to find me over Christmas and then didn't stop and was so weird when I went over for dinner. I think he wants to do the right thing. He just doesn't know how. He never went to Dad School. He went to Plant Growing School, and that's where he's a genius, because he could study it and learn all about it. One thing though, he managed NOT to call me Smartass even once that afternoon.

I think my mom must have had some serious damage done to her when she was very young. Her whole life seems to be devoted to Dad. There's just no other explanation. I can see his attraction to her — she's very plant-like. Keep her watered and in the sun a few hours a day and she's happy. And, yes, maybe my sister'll grow up to be a decent person. I hope so. Although I'm afraid she might grow up to be a plant too.

Speaking of 50 below, it's been exactly that here too — and another reason I'm leaving now (I'm running out of wood ALREADY).

So that's it in a nutshell. You know my plan. The rest of the letter will catch you up on the latest, and why I'm leaving now.

(End of the section written after what's coming up, which was written a couple of days ago. So that's why it has its own date and brand new paper and doesn't just continue from this page. Make sense?)

Sweeny

Dear Jessica:

The most amazing thing happened today. I almost want to ask, "What the heck were you doing?" And then, "What the heck were you doing HERE?"

All right, I know, back up.

Gladys and Ron have kind of adopted me lately. Ron is Gladys's brother who's in his early sixties I guess and runs the garage part of the Stone's Throw.

At any rate, Ron's the guy who's got The Beast running again (a rebuilt starter and battery) and is one of those guys who is always doing something involving grease or metal or welding torches, except when he's fishing. Gladys says he used to be a drinker but he's on the wagon now and has been for thirteen years. I'd say he's pretty well got it licked because he's very into AA and holds meetings in the church hall every week.

Anyway, Ron has built a fish hut on metal skids. I don't know if you're familiar with ice-fishing, but it's a common practice here. People use fish huts to get away from their wives and do a lot of drinking. After the ice has frozen hard the lake is suddenly dotted with huts and tents containing a fisher or two, flanked by skidoos and pick-ups. This is especially true on weekends, but even during the week a local or two is parked on the ice huddled in his hut. I shouldn't just say "his" because a lot of women do this too — like Gladys on Mondays when she closes the café and can get someone to look after the store.

Today Ron asked me if I wanted to go ice-fishing with him. Not being especially busy I said sure, and before I knew it I was sitting on the back of his old snowmobile with his hut sliding behind us crossing the lake.

Anyway, we stopped at a secluded bay. There was nothing around but expanses of snow-covered ice. The low hills rose off the uninhabited lakeshore and a gray sky hung above. There was not a speck of color anywhere. No wind.

I helped Ron with the auger which we had trouble starting. After about the thirtieth pull, it starts and we growl a hole in the ice, spitting and chewing like some evil hungry thing, scrape aside the loose ice and slush with a shovel, then pull the hut over top. Then we drop our lines through the hole quick before it freezes up. Before WE freeze up too.

Ron doesn't talk a lot. It's like he only owns a few words and doesn't like to waste them. Every now and then he'll say "Yep," even though no one's asked him anything. It's one of the words he has extra.

We were sitting inside all warm and comfy (except for Ron's tobacco smoke) with our lines dangling (you can actually see the lake bottom and the fish inspecting your bait) when I decided I needed to relieve myself.

APART

"Yep," Ron said before I even began to move for the door.

One of the advantages of being a guy is there aren't many limits on where you can empty your bladder. As long as it's not upwind and you aren't exposing yourself to charges of public indecency, you're pretty well free. It's actually a cool feeling to point yourself into the great outdoors and watch the steaming stream arc from your body like a fountain.

Except when a bear is watching you.

At first I didn't know it was a bear. It was a dark figure near the shore. I thought, "Maybe it's a dog, but it doesn't move like a dog, and is too big to be a dog, too fat to be a deer, and too short to be a moose. It is a bear. But what's a bear doing out at this time of year? It can't be a bear!" All these thoughts took place in a lot less time than it took me to zip up my pants.

But yes, it was a bear and it was coming right at me.

I yelled for Ron to come out.

"Yep," he said, and came stumbling out of the hut.

I pointed and Ron strung together the most words I've heard him use in the few weeks I've known him.

"Holy shit!" he said. "Bear!"

Now if this were a novel or something, it would be a good place to have a chapter break, just to keep you reading. So I'll insert a little pause here, in case you want to go the bathroom or refill your cup of tea. Do you drink tea? I have this vision of you drinking tea, with one hand holding the cup, the other holding back your hair from getting in the tea. You do this subconsciously and it's quite attractive — mostly because you're so unaware of it.

Timmy would be doing something really quiet like sitting there rocking, deep in thought, deep into those places he goes. Maybe you read bits and pieces to him and he says, "Don't throw that Sween in the garbage." Or at least that's what I hope he would say, if he said anything at all.

Anyway, back to the bear.

Bears can move at a pretty good clip and he's getting closer. It's quite clear we are the bear's destination. The question is, why?

Ron picks up the shovel. He climbs on top of the snowmobile and starts yelling, roaring really.

The bear stops. He's still about a hundred meters away. It looks like he's thinking it over. He takes a few paces off to the side, then he turns and starts galloping toward us again.

It's about now I start getting scared. He's not a real big bear, and I'm not even sure he's a he, but he looks like he could do a fair bit of damage if all you've got is one shovel between the two of you.

When he gets to us, he slows down as if to size up which one of us he is going to go after first. He walks by the hut, swats it, just about tips it over. He's showing off what he can do. Ron's got some frozen bait in a small plastic bucket. The bear swats that. It flies over top of the hut. He starts coming toward me. Ron swings the shovel and smacks the bear across the nose. The bear sits down for a second, stunned.

Ron's got his attention. The bear gets up and starts toward Ron.

I look around for something to hit him with. I pick up the

auger. You can't swing an auger, it's too heavy. I pull the cord and it roars to life. I hold the roaring auger over my head as though I am suddenly very big and loud. The bear takes one look, backs off a few paces.

Ron swings the shovel again, bonking him on the head. The bear turns and gallops back the way he came.

Ron and I aren't much interested in fishing any more. And while we pack up the hut and all the fishing gear, the bear paces up and down the shore. He does not go into the woods or wherever it was he came from. He/she is still there when we leave.

Bears are supposed to be hibernating now. Why did this one come out? Maybe we disturbed it when we were augering the hole in the ice. (Although I don't see how — we were a long way offshore.) Maybe he was sick. Maybe his internal clock was all screwed up. (I'd be mad too if I woke up in the middle of winter when I thought it should be spring.) Maybe he was hungry and didn't get enough to eat in the fall and his stomach was really grumbling. (There were a lot of fires around here last year so food was probably scarce.)

Maybe he was she.

Maybe she was you.

Something, whatever it is, is definitely wrong. That's why I'll soon be on my way.

Sooner than later,

Sween

Dear Sween:

I wonder where you will read this letter, and how long it will take you to reach it. I hope — wherever it is — that you are okay.

As I said in my last letter, I really admire you for going out on your own and making your own destiny. I hope the Beast cooperates. You've chosen the worst possible season for driving east, but I'm sure you're aware of that. I suppose normal people head south in winter if they can. But then, "normal" seems to be something you and I are naturally good at avoiding. And I think that's fine, although we both know just how much courage it takes to be out on a limb, with plenty of people ready to say I told you so if we crash.

We won't fall, Sween. Or if we do, I think our own willpower and imagination will help us rise up again. When I was a bit younger and I heard the French national anthem for the first time, I got really excited, particularly over the words: "Contre nous de la tyrannie," and then the rousing "Marchons" of the chorus. Which translates roughly, The tyrants are against us, but we are going to beat them by marching together. That just seemed such a powerful idea to me. That people who are ground down could free themselves by joining together in spirit. I still get goosebumps thinking of that possibility for every human being.

I know we're not oppressed in the terrible way many people are, but staying true to your dreams and following your own path still takes some doing. When you describe your mom as plant-like, I see what I don't want to be. Just like I don't want to be besotted with a jerk the way my mom is with Gunner.

It's great that you have a new starter motor and tires that can handle the road. I hope you also have flares and a box or two of raisins in the car in case you get stuck somewhere. (Why on earth did I write that?) Above all, I don't want you to get stuck.

I told Great-Grandma what you're doing and she said, "That boy's got smeddum." This Scots word packs a lot of meaning, and it is extremely positive even though it might not sound that way. If you've got smeddum, you're armed with courage and common sense too.

You're certainly determined and resourceful, Sween, and I really look forward to meeting you finally. Of course you are welcome here.

I finally told my mom about you, and she says you can stay with us. There are plenty of rooms in this old farmhouse. Mom really likes the fact I have a friend. She says she worries that I am too cut off socially.

She came back from her stay in Fredericton at Mrs. Oliphant's a few days ago. The plan is for Mom and Timmy to move down there to join Gunner in the fall, once he's got some savings behind him. (This is Gunner?) I hope to have started at university by then if all goes according to my own plan.

What a lot of changes! It is hard for me to get my head around them, especially the idea of being away from Timmy and Great-Grandma.

I've thought a lot about your encounter with the bear. Of course I am very glad that no one was hurt — either you or Ron or the bear.

I am pretty sure this strange incident has absolutely nothing to do with me. Everything is miraculously fine here. Mom is happy at the idea of moving in six months or so and being with Gunner. She says Mrs. Oliphant is checking into good school possibilities for Timmy, and I guess I will have to trust that she is as good a person as Mom seems to think.

Mrs. Oliphant certainly seems to have no shortage of money. According to Mom she is a very well-preserved fifty-year-old with exquisite manners. Doesn't well-preserved make you think of pickles?

As far as Lancelot is concerned, I did tell Mom about the threatening phone calls, and she called Gunner who blew a gasket. I suppose this shows he still cares about us. Anyway, Gunner said he would call his old pal Snorter (I think I've mentioned him before).

Snorter is a very big man who wouldn't look at all out of place in a documentary about Cro-Magnon man. I am not meaning to be unkind here. He really enjoys terrifying people, and he does a very good job at it. And yes, he does snort.

So, Snorter was dispatched to "have a word" with Lancelot, and things have been quiet ever since.

I am enclosing a money order made out to you for fifty dollars. One of the great things that happened to me recently was that I won $200 as a prize in a short story competition. That's why I can afford to send you $50 now, and more later once I hear from you again and know where you are headed next. You can use the money for gas, or to buy yourself a few hot meals.

The story I wrote was called "The Sea Bridge" and it was based on Great-Grandma's description of her homesickness for Scotland when she first moved to Canada. Remember I told you she said she would have walked home over the Atlantic if there had been a bridge?

When I won first prize, she was as "proud as punch" as she likes to say. Mom was pleased too, but in a much more muted way. I think that's because she is following Gunner's line in encouraging me to go into business studies, not English.

Back to the bear. I wonder if you and Ron might have unknowingly disturbed a sacred place, and the bear then appeared to make you aware you were trespassing (in a manner of speaking). Reading your description of the auger in the ice "spitting and chewing like some evil hungry thing," I think you were subliminally aware that you and Ron were intruding on a holy place. Perhaps that secluded bay has a spirit of quietness that must not be fractured. Perhaps the hibernating bear woke up to make that point clear to you.

The experience belongs to you, and you know best how to interpret it. But as I said, I really don't think the bear's appearance has anything to do with me or Timmy, unless it's a harbinger of things to come. And I certainly hope not.

By the way, Timmy likes the photograph you sent of you

and Zamboni, except that he keeps asking what happened to your hair, and why "Sween has a plain head."

"Sween will wear his plain head, Juss?"

"No, Timmy," I tell him, "Sween has grown his hair back now." He doesn't quite understand how hair grows or why he needs to get his cut every now and then. Mom does it for him at the kitchen table, and when Timmy sees the scissors come out, he can sometimes create quite a big scene. We both hope you have a warm hat and gloves too, for your drive through Manitoba and Ontario and Quebec. What a long way it looks on the map. But I suppose it's like any other big task, and you'll accomplish it a bit at a time.

I believe I can feel you getting closer.

I am praying that you avoid blizzards and freezing rain, and that your car radio works so that you can check on the weather coming your way.

Your admiring friend in the East,

Jessica

P.S. I'm not a big tea drinker, although Great-Grandma is. She always has a pot of tea in a glass carafe brewing away on the stove. What I really love is espresso. So one of the things I've bought myself with the money I won was one of those little metal Italian coffee pots that goes right on the stove and bubbles up a wickedly potent drink. Gunner says it's an affectation (not the word he used) so I know I must be on to a good thing! ("Putting on the dog" was what he actually said.)

February 20

Dear Jess:

As you can see by the postmark, I haven't gotten too far. I don't know if your letter is waiting at the General Delivery boxes in any of the places I had hoped to be by now — or if I will ever get to them.

I feel guilty about not coming and sort of leaving you in an unexpected lurch. It was a dumb idea anyway. Whatever would I do in Matagouche? Dumb, dumb, dumb. What was I thinking?

I'm not myself. Or maybe I am myself and I wish I wasn't. Whatever.

This is what happened.

I left the lake and was actually driving in my car packed with my worldly belongings which wasn't a lot, with the tape deck blasting full volume, along with the heater blower (it was 30 below). I don't know which made more noise — the old tape deck or the heater blower.

It was early afternoon, bright and sunny. I'd just rounded a curve in the highway when what should trot out of the woods but a coyote. She was small with a lot of red on her. A moment later another emerged — big blue-coat. They both turned and ran back into the woods. It was right about the spot where I saw one drag itself from the road after I hit it that night just after Christmas.

I was suddenly filled with this feeling of overwhelming sadness. I started crying. Sobbing. I couldn't stop. This went on and on. The road was blurry. I looked at my speedometer. I was doing 180 kms per hour.

I tried to slow down.

I kept crying.

I slowed to 150.

It didn't take too long to get to town. I slowed to the speed limit.

I drove straight to the hospital emergency. I told them the obvious, that I couldn't stop crying. They checked me into the psych ward.

So now I'm medicated and calm.

I'm no longer crying.

But I don't know what I'm going to do.

I'm back in my parents' basement. They tiptoe around me like I'm a nut-case — which I guess I am. The shrink says I'm bi-polar. Great.

There's no question I'm a bit weird right now — to use one of your words. But the days get longer and sometimes I feel almost normal.

Sorry if you find this upsetting. I did try to phone you, but

APART

that number you gave didn't work. A recording said, "No longer in service or is disconnected." I hope you just copied it down wrong.

I'll shut up now.

Your crazy friend,

Sween

Dear Sween:

I really hope you are feeling better when this letter gets to you. I am thinking of you all the time. My heart goes out to you — or at least it would if I didn't need all my resources here for myself at the moment.

Your letter came as a big shock to me. But then I suppose the whole situation of crying non-stop and finding yourself driving at 180 kilometers an hour (thank God your instinct kicked in and you slowed down and got yourself to a hospital) came as a colossal shock to you too.

It seems there's nothing more gigantic in our lives than our emotions. They can certainly wham and bang us around. I think it's a terrifically positive sign that you saw the little reddish coyote and the big blue-coat just about where the other coyote was hit. This shows his spirit is still with you, as Elaine said.

I am sure you are going to be all right. You have too much courage and talent and sensitivity not to bounce back and up, no matter what it is that's distressing you.

I don't want you to think I am being surfacey or insensitive here, smothering you with a lot of meaningless upbeat words. The fact is I am in a big emotional mess myself. I didn't want to tell you my troubles when you obviously have plenty of your own.

In fact, I just tore up a letter I wrote to you about an hour ago — one where I pretended that everything is hunky-dory here in the old farmhouse in Matagouche. But then my conscience gave me a prick, and I decided you need an honest account of what is happening to me, and the really bad situation that is threatening Timmy.

You'll have guessed that "bad situation" equals Gunner.

I hate my father more than ever. I really didn't think that was possible, but perhaps hatred is a bottomless pit and you can always go deeper.

He got fired from his chauffeur job, of course. I knew it wouldn't last. Gunner is too full of himself to be a uniformed lackey for very long. The upshot is that he's back, with some of the most dangerous ideas he's come up with yet.

First, he is dealing drugs again. He has done time for this before, and the fact is he is putting us all at risk. I know he's dealing, and Mom knows too, but she is swallowing his line that he's aware of all the possible pitfalls this time. He's not going to get caught and he's going to make a big profit and then take Mom to Costa Rica by way of New Orleans and Mexico. As I understand it, they are never coming back.

I haven't told you the worst part. He's going to put Timmy in a "home." He says he's checked into it and there is a great residence for autistic kids in Maine (for God's sake) and that he is taking Timmy there at the end of next month.

The idea of Timmy being sent away makes me feel sick to my stomach. It fills me with a boiling rage at Gunner and a terrible deep-down fear for Timmy.

I am still trying to figure out how I can stop this. I know what these "homes" are like, particularly if Gunner is choosing it. They'll tie Timmy to his bed or a chair if he acts up. No one will read to him or care about him or try to understand what he's saying. I can't even make myself write down some of the worst things I fear might happen to him.

I asked Great-Grandma to speak to Gunner, and she did try to persuade him that this "home" is really a bad idea for Timmy's future. Apparently he told her that Timmy hasn't got a future. "Let's face it," he said. "He can't develop. He's never going to be anything more than a drain on all of us."

Then he gave Great-Granny some line about how Timmy's needs are wearing Mom down, and that she is on the edge of a nervous breakdown. He also told her that Timmy has started playing with himself in public and that he is turning into "a real problem and an embarrassment to the family."

This is all bullshit, and look who's talking about being an embarrassment. But Gunner is a great manipulator as well as a really good liar. He knows Great-Grandma has a strong prudish streak, and that the idea of one of her great-grand-children doing "something degrading" in public will really disgust and upset her.

Of course, the atmosphere in the house has been explosive

and depressing since Gunner got back. Timmy is wetting the bed regularly again. And he's wearing his earmuffs indoors all the time.

And then to make matters worse, Timmy walked off with a big chunk of hash that Gunner had been dumb enough to leave on the coffee table in the living-room. The hashish is a deep chocolate brown so maybe it looked like fudge. It has a gold embossed pattern on it, and that would attract Timmy as well.

So when the hashish (worth about $1,000) went missing, things got really bad. Gunner was just about frothing at the mouth. First he accused me of taking it, although I don't know what he thought I would do with it if I value my life at all. Then he started interrogating Timmy, shaking him and making him wail, and me feel ill and wild at the same time.

It was Snorter who saved the day by showing up just when Gunner was starting to lose it totally. I was actually poised to kick Gunner in the nuts at that point, as you suggested. Fortunately Snorter managed to cool Gunner out, and I took Timmy to his room and got him calmed down.

When Timmy seemed okay for questions, I asked him where he put Gunner's chunk of brown stuff with the gold letters. He showed me right away. It was tucked inside a tear in the fabric of his old stuffed toy dog. Thank God he didn't try to take the plastic wrap off and eat some.

But for Gunner that episode absolutely confirmed that Timmy belongs in a "home."

Every time I go to open my mouth about Timmy, Gunner just about snaps my head off. "Shut it, granny-girl. All you've done with that kid is keep a hopeless case going longer than it needs to."

So that's how things are here, Sween. I'm crying too, and I'm not sleeping well. I'm considering taking Timmy and running off. I don't know where we would go or what we would live on, but it may come to that. And I don't even have Great-Grandma as an ally now.

It's just Timmy and me up against my stupid father.

I tried talking to Mr. Powys about it, and he spoke with his wife. (Remember I told you she is a social worker?) Apparently Gunner is "within his rights" to do this because he is Timmy's father. And that is such a cosmic joke because Gunner has never done anything fatherly for Timmy in his entire life.

The fact is he wants rid of both of us. He bought me a cheap cardboard suitcase so that I can move all my things to Great-Grandma's once Timmy's gone and Mom and Gunner head off to New Orleans on the ElectraGlide.

By the way, I am sorry our phone was cut off when you called. Gunner yanked the cord out of the wall one day when he was having a fit about the line being tapped. He's getting paranoid on top of everything else.

I did try to phone you from Great-Grandma's. Whoever answered (your mother?) told me you weren't able to come to the phone — whatever that meant. But it's probably just as well because I'm not sure what I would have said or been able to say before gushing into some muddle of tears, embarrassing myself and you.

APART

Pray for Timmy, and for me to find a way to stop Gunner somehow, even if it doesn't come naturally to you to do so. I don't know who else to ask to pray for us.

Love,

Jessica

March 4

Dear Jessica:

Wow! Record turnaround time. It's been five days since you mailed your letter. Postes Canada Post has really turned on the afterburners. Do you suppose they sense the urgency of our correspondence?

I'm slowly crawling out of my hole — the hole being quite literally my parents' basement. I decided (with the aid of appropriate medication and hours of chatting with my shrink) to try go back to school. THAT lasted about twenty minutes. I walked down the hall to the principal's office and almost was physically ill. I couldn't do it. Not this time anyways. I literally walked in one door and out the other. You know what got me most? The smell — of chalk dust and that closet where you keep old stuff. It made me gag.

My sense of smell is really strong. Must be the meds. Or maybe I'm turning into Coyote. Canines have extra-sensitive noses, right? I suppose that would also explain all the hair growing on my back too. I'm kidding, I'm kidding.

I must say, I laughed out loud when you said Timmy stole Gunner's hash. You are lucky he didn't think it was a Mars bar and scoff the thing whole. On the one hand, it would probably have killed him, but on the other, it wouldn't have been a bad way to go. I know that's not a very nice thing to say, but I do believe it would be better than being shackled to a bedstead somewhere in the State of Maine.

Although you IMPLY that you returned the hashish to Gunner, you didn't actually say so. Am I reading between the lines that Snorter calmed him down enough that he forgot about it? That you have now hidden the stuff yourself, waiting for an opportune time to park it on Gunner when the local RCM Police are checking to see if his bike plates are legal? Or why they are not on his bike? Having been mysteriously removed by some mysterious agent?

Sounds like a good plan to me. Just think how pleasant things would be if he was in jail! I might even continue my trip east if I could help do this. Lord knows I'm not going to survive long in this basement — especially since my only friend is gone.

Yesterday I took dear old Zamboni for a walk. It was a short walk. He doesn't have a lot of energy and the trip around the block pretty well exhausts him. He seems to be in pretty good spirits despite the growth on his neck. He's always been affectionate and likes to get physically close to you. Except now he's quite repulsive. He not only looks like he's getting ready to kick the bucket, he smells like he's jumped into that bucket and it's not filled with anything you want to put your nose near. He stinks. Like a sackful of dirty socks. Again, my sense of smell is really strong.

But I must be getting better because my dad called me Smartass today — the first time in a long time. I just about hugged him. It's funny how you get used to "normal," or what you think normal should be, and how you miss it when it's gone. At any rate, the reason he called me that was because I suggested he use part of his million dollar research grant to find a cure for Zamboni. He didn't think my suggestion appropriate.

Anyway, Zamboni has not responded to the puppy dog version of chemotherapy. At least he didn't lose all his hair. But he will not be with us long. Till tomorrow in fact, when Dad will take him to the vet and everyone will stand around and say goodbye. Suzanne will cry. Mom will pat her hand, and Dad will say something really intelligent like, "He was a real good dog."

I won't be there. Zamboni and I said our goodbyes today.

If dogs could talk, Boni wouldn't have a large vocabulary. His most frequent phrase would be "I'm happy." That would apply for just about everything. The next phrase would be "I'm sad," which he says only when you don't take him for a walk, or with you in the car. That's it. That's the extent of his vocab.

But today he put them both together. "I'm happy/sad," he said. He can be pretty eloquent with such a few words.

If dogs can pray, they must get their prayers answered a lot. But then, they don't ask for much — a few kibbles, a warm place to sleep and a pat on the head every now and then. I admit I don't do much of that — praying. I used to when I was little but I gave it up. It just got too confusing. Either I was asking for favors or whining about not getting them. It was about getting my way, what I wanted.

What about God? I mean, what are his plans? (Okay, I know He might be a She — but just for sake of convention…) You know what? I can't believe our plans would ever be the same. Not only does he have the whole rest of the planet to look after, he's got the whole universe — that's the KNOWN universe. What about AND BEYOND?? My little problems don't amount to a hill of beans as Bogey said to Ilsa.

But because you asked, I prayed. For Timmy.

I'm hoping this letter gets to you as fast as yours got to me so that I can find out about the missing hash. In the meantime, I'll work on keeping my eyes on the horizon — so I don't get landsick. I looked up Matagouche again. Whereas I am in the Middle of Nowhere, you are on the Edge of it. I may show up yet.

As ever,

Sween

March 12

Dear Sween:

I hope you get this letter as quickly as I got yours. Maybe you're right. Maybe Canada Post does have a heart, and understands that we need to communicate at top speed right now.

Sometimes I wonder if our correspondence would be different if we could e-mail each other. Would that change the way we wrote each other, do you think? But since we still don't even have a working phone here, my getting e-mail is about as likely as Gunner turning to religion.

I want to say how sorry I am about Zamboni. Your happy/sad description of his last day with you is an eloquent and fine tribute to him. I am sure you will keep him alive and well and bounding about joyfully in your memory.

And thanks so much for your prayer for Timmy. I really appreciate it, especially since you are obviously not too big on praying. I do understand, believe me. But these are desperate times, and if we are going to pray at all, I think it's always a good idea to do it for somebody else.

My good news (in a manner of speaking) is that the

APART

mighty Gunner is temporarily disabled. He fell down the rickety old basement stairs and landed on his shoulder with his arm folded under him at an odd angle. He hasn't broken any bones, but he has sprained his left wrist and he's sprained his right arm badly. It is all bound up in elastic bandage, held together with little metal clips. He holds the trussed-up arm against his chest like Napoleon and puts on his feel-sorry-for-me expression.

He moans a lot and is taking heavy-duty pain killers with codeine. Plus he is smoking all the hashish he's supposed to be selling. All these drugs have the great advantage of putting him to sleep for quite a few hours during the day. I am sorry he is in pain, but also not at all sorry, if you know what I mean.

I think feelings of vengeance, and delight at other people's pain, even if it's Gunner's pain, are dangerous and degrading emotions. Look where vengeance leads in Shakespeare's plays, with a stage full of dead bodies and some minor, boring character delivering the final words. Look where vengeance has got the poor old world right now.

So, I have to struggle not to be happy that my father is in severe discomfort.

What I am happy about is that this puts him out of commission in terms of driving Timmy down to Maine — or driving anywhere — for at least the next four weeks.

This also means I've got some time to try to help Timmy somehow. By the way, Gunner asked Snorter if he would take Timmy to the home in Maine, and Snorter refused outright.

In fact, he looked really upset at the idea. And Snorter is not the kind of man who often looks upset. It's funny that even though he frequently looks and sounds like Cro-Magnon man, he is actually far more sensitive and compassionate than Gunner will ever be.

I will never forget how he cooled Gunner down about Timmy walking off with the lump of hash. In your letter you said Timmy "stole" the hash, but I don't think he understands the concept of theft. I've had to work very hard with him to get across the idea that he must not take other kids' things at school, and that just because he likes the look of somebody else's comic book, for example, he can't just pick it up and walk off with it.

Back to Gunner's hash stash (and yes, I gave it back to him, and there's more in the house than just that one chunk). It's a very good thing that Timmy didn't eat any of it, because if he had, he would probably be psychotic now as well as autistic.

Here's what I've done so far with the extra time Gunner's accident has given me. First I went to talk to the teachers at Timmy's day program to get to the bottom of Gunner's story that Timmy has been exposing and playing with himself. As I suspected, this is absolutely untrue. In fact, they were surprised to hear "our father" was back.

Then I visited Great-Granny and managed to persuade her that Gunner had made it all up about Timmy so that he could justify putting him away. So now Timmy and I have her back on our side, which is wonderful. I think Gunner is a bit afraid of her, even though he wouldn't admit it. She is the only one still living of all his forebears, and I think her high standards are a mirror he finds it hard to look into.

I also talked again to Mr. Powys and his wife about the "home" in Maine. Unfortunately there is not a lot they can tell me because I don't have the name of the home or even exactly where it is or if it is regulated or not. And Gunner isn't telling.

I appreciate your suggestion, by the way, about setting the RCMP on to Gunner and his hash stash, but even though I despise him, I couldn't do that.

Jail warps people. Gunner did eight months in prison when I was ten, and he came out a different man — harder, meaner, far more cynical and ready to use people in a cruel way. I am sure he was kinder to me before his jail time. He never called me Sourface until after his prison experience.

At any rate, I know enough to realize prison is not a fate I want for him. I am sure there are other ways to stop him from taking Timmy to Maine.

It would be great to see you, Sween. You and your tent and your calico car. I did send a letter to Kenora so perhaps it will still be waiting for you if you do come East.

Your happy/sad friend in N.B.,

Jessica

April 16

Dear Jessica:

I have no real excuses for not writing. I have been "busy."
Isn't that what people say when they've been neglecting their
friends? What that actually means is that I've been so totally
taken up with my own little problems that I can't even see
beyond my own very limited horizon. (Not literally of
course. I'm still in Saskatchewan where the horizon is actually below your feet — whether or not you're lying down.)

I got a job. At a golf course.

I'm writing you today because it's snowing out. Not just
snowing, it's blizzarding. You can't mow much grass in the
snow — not that we're mowing any grass yet anyway — but
it's too miserable to do ANYTHING outside. I'm supposedly in the machine shop painting little blocks of wood that are
the front tee markers here. But I'm done that and no one's
around to crack the whip. So that explains the globby bits of
red paint on the paper. It's not blood. Although it might as
well be. I never realized how much work there is to do on a
golf course. You drive by one and it all looks so neat and tidy.
Well, there are a dozen or so guys making it look that way.

APART

• • •

It's a bit later now, and I'm at "home." I got caught writing this afternoon by Reg. He gave me two more buckets of paint (one blue and one white) and seventy-two more blocks of wood. I now look like the American flag. Yippee.

Reg is the greenskeeper and a retired cop. He was one of those sensitive cops who went around to the schools in a van telling kids about the dangers of drug addiction and always to cross at the crosswalks — as though the two were somehow related. When I say "sensitive" I mean "for a cop." He wasn't into breaking heads or dropping my native brothers out in the boonies near the power plant when it's thirty below, but Mr. Personality he is not. Just my boss, and apparently a childhood friend of my father's. If you are beginning to see a picture here, it is because there is one. Yes, my dad got me the job.

The good part (if there is a good part) is that the "home" I keep putting in quotes is a thirty-foot trailer located in Reg's brother's farmyard. There is nothing else in the yard but two grain bins and a machine shed. Reg's brother (Geoff) lives in the city. So I have my own place which is only a slight improvement on my parents' basement in some ways, but a great relief in others. For example, I have no running water here at the moment and if you recall my heightened sense of smell I am not a great picnic to be around — not even to me. Fortunately I can shower in the members' locker room at the golf course — until the members show up, that is. Still, it is my own place. I even pay rent.

So aside from working and sleeping, I don't do much — except play pool. There's a place I go called Cute Ips, which is supposedly a pool joint for those of the female persuasion (I'm sure you'd like it) but I hardly ever see any girls here. They're all too intimidated by the owner's daughter who runs the place. She has the same personality as Reg (so I'm kind of used to it). Her name is Camilla, and like her horsey namesake, Prince Charles' wife, she'll never win any beauty contests.

At any rate, I'm kind of getting good at pool. I seem to have a knack for it. Camilla wants me to enter a tourney here this weekend for unranked players.

I might. If I survive the bikers tonight.

Perhaps I should explain.

Three of them came in last Thursday complete with black leather vests, scary hair and tattoos. At any rate, I was practicing on a table by myself (Camilla gives me special rates) when one of them challenged me.

Well, I beat him. Then I beat him again. Then I beat his buddy. Then I beat his buddy again. Then I beat his buddy's buddy. Then I lost. But all three of them accused me of throwing the game — which, of course, I did.

So that's how come I have a game tonight. They're bringing a friend of theirs to play me. I'm really nervous. What happens if I beat him? I have to wait till 10:30 to find out. That's way past my bed time. (I've been hitting the hay early — it's the meds AND the exercise.) I wasn't able to have a shower after work so I'm still red, white and blue. I look like my car. Maybe they'll just feel sorry for me and leave me alone.

APART

So, does Gunner play pool? I guess it depends on how he holds his cue stick and which arm is broken. There's this old guy who comes into Ips and plays sometimes — a vet, I guess. He's only got one arm but he shoots pretty well. He never has to talc his hook.

I'll mail this on the way to meet my destiny tonight. You'll have to wait to find out what — if anything — happens. Camilla has a little boy, Tyler, who she lets have the run of the place (and why not). He has a little stool he stands on so he can reach the tables and shoot using a full-size adult cue. He drags the stool around with him and he's already better than a lot of people I know. But he is still such a little kid. For some reason he reminds me of Timmy. "I'm a dragon," he says to anyone he meets. Apparently Camilla told him he was born in the year of the dragon. He's very proud of this.

So guess who also works at the golf course? Coyote, naturally. He's in charge of pest control — unofficially that is. I haven't seen a mate yet, but I'm sure there's one around. Lots of food to raise a family with. The place is overrun by gophers.

You take care. I think of you lots.

Sincerely,

James Charles MacSween

Dear Sween:

I am really sorry I didn't get a chance to reply to your letter right away. But I've been thinking about you a lot, wondering how your game with the pool champ went.

I hope things turned out well and that you still have all your teeth and useful appendages. I am sure you are okay because you have some good and helpful spirits around you, including Camilla the horse, Tyler the dragon and, of course, Coyote.

I still marvel at your ability to transform and adapt to all kinds of situations with a new self. Now you've got a 30-foot trailer, a painted body and a newly discovered talent for playing pool. I guess you and Coyote share this ability to take on new shapes. This is a great talent for a writer to have, Sween. Are you still writing, by the way — other than the letters you send to me, I mean?

Back to pool. Gunner plays and so does Snorter. They have a reputation locally so to make money on a game they have to travel to Campbellton or even Fredericton, where people don't know them.

As for golf, Snorter says it's a "snub" game. He means snob.

Snorter has a bit of a speech impediment. But this doesn't matter at all because I am seeing more and more fine qualities in him all the time. He has been a real support to me and Timmy, speaking up for us when Gunner gets especially nasty.

Which is so, so often these days.

Gunner's arm is still healing, so he still can't drive (the good part from Timmy's and my viewpoint). But the fact that he can't drive, particularly his beloved bike, makes him cranky as hell.

He is even meaner when he is restless and can't go bombing down the road. A meaner-than-usual Gunner makes for a very tense household. Timmy's little face looks so strained. He keeps clenching his fists and pushing them into his cheeks and moving his head back and forth in an agitated way.

Mom is not in great shape emotionally either, as it seems Gunner is up to his old tricks again. He has been going to see a physiotherapist at a sports clinic for help with his arm. The physiotherapist is younger than Mom and very, very pretty and fit. You can guess the rest.

Gossip travels fast around here and it didn't take long for Mom to hear that Gunner and the physiotherapist (her name is Linda) had been spotted necking outside the clinic.

He denied it at first. Then he admitted it (sort of). Then he denied it again.

What a jerk he is! What a pig! I overheard him boasting to Snorter about how hard Linda has fallen for him (he put it a bit more crudely than that) so I know for sure he is cheating on Mom again.

Mom's crying a lot. But she is managing to stay off the

pills and booze this time. And she is still going to work at the salon. I am really proud of her.

In the meantime, I am trying to focus on getting ready for exams and keep my mind fixed on my own goals.

Yesterday afternoon things got even worse around here.

I was alone with Timmy when the RCMP officers (yes, there were two of them) made their visit. When I saw the cruiser coming down our laneway, I had time to fly down the stairs and check for evidence of Gunner's dope smoking, including rolling papers. My training in these matters goes way back: "Never open the door to the Grook without having a good look around the house first." (Gunner and Snorter refer to the RCMP as the Grook because the force's initials in French are GRC.)

Well, it turns out these two Grooks were making their call on Mrs. Oliphant's behalf. Apparently some valuable objects are missing, and she's named Gunner as a suspect.

Naturally, this has put him in an even more foul mood.

"That old hag," he said. "She had the hots for me and I wasn't up for it. That's what this is all about. Her scraggy old neck was enough to put me off."

He was so full of himself, I nearly laughed.

Unfortunately, he caught me trying to control a smirk.

"You think this is funny, granny girl? You think it's amusing that Mrs. Goddamn Oliphant is trying to have me put away?"

Then I did something really stupid. I said, "Well, isn't that what you're trying to do to Timmy?"

"You miserable little bitch!" he screamed at me. And he was so furious that he forgot about his injured arm and took a swing at me.

His yowl of pain was demonic, and his face went so white, I almost felt sorry for him.

So Gunner's back on the painkillers, his physiotherapy has been suspended, and I'm in the doghouse. Mom is really mad at me for "provoking" him. But secretly I believe he got precisely what he deserved.

Snorter's been kind to me though. He even offered me some uppers to help me study longer. I had the sense to say no thank you, of course. I've seen Gunner coming down from amphetamines and it's ugly.

So, inadvertently, I've managed to buy Timmy some more time. Which is a very good thing. Because Snorter let drop something when I asked him if he and Gunner had ever actually seen the home.

"It smells real bad, Jessica." He wouldn't say any more, but he looked so worried, I got more scared than ever for Timmy.

That's the way it is here in Matagouche.

Let's hope the best for each other, as always.

Your loyal friend in the East,

Jessica

P.S. You signed your last letter with your full name. Is there a reason you did that? Are you no longer Sween?

Dear Jessica:

The reason I signed my full name was just in case you forgot who I was — it had been so long. Or maybe it was to remind me who I am. I don't know. Every now and then I feel the need to write my name in full, just to see what it looks like. Or what it WOULD look like, say on a diploma or degree. I don't plan on being stupid and uneducated forever. I will go back and finish high school some time.

Just not right now. I'm too busy. First of course — on the course — I'm fixing broken water pipes (the frost heaves the pipes underground and they break) which is a dirty, messy, clay-ridden job that I seem to be good at, and Reg (remember Reg?) keeps me covered in mud repairing them. I can't tell if it's a pat on the back or a kick in the pants, but that's what I do all day — that and other odd jobs like raking and painting and moving sod. Soon it'll be mowing, mowing and more mowing. Eight hours a day.

The other thing I'm doing is pool. After work. I was going to write you immediately after my adventure with the bikers, but I got caught up in the tournament the next day and, well, you know how one thing leads to another. Before you know it a week has passed and there sitting in the mail box is another letter from you to which I am now responding.

Anyway, the three bikers show up at Ips and with them is a fourth, and she's a girl. Perhaps girl isn't the right word. She definitely has all the trimmings of a female, but she is bigger than the bikers and looks like she could use a shave.

She says two words to me. "Rack 'em." Which I do. Then she clears the whole table off the break.

I rack the balls again. She breaks but nothing goes down. I shoot and miss. Then she clears the table again. She throws her cue onto the table, turns and walks out. The bikers follow. Smirking.

I still don't know if she was a she or some guy in drag. Anyway, I have all my fingers and toes.

I got one shot. One. It was incredible. I was so shaken that when Camilla's little dragon Tyler wanted to play, he almost beat me too.

So when I went to the tourney the following night, I lost my first game. I made a few shots, but just couldn't get any shape. I finished third on the B side, which isn't too bad. At least I kind of know where I stand. It's interesting to watch the really good players and how they put spin on the ball, moving it around things and off the rail, keeping it in the middle of the table. I'm still at the stage of trying to get the ball to go in a straight line consistently. I'm learning though and have a good knack for angles.

Guess what I found in Geoff's machine shed? Under a

dusty blue tarp was a bike — a motorcycle — a '79 Honda Gold Wing, 1000 cc. I put some fresh gas in it, changed the oil and jump started it and it roared to life!

Anyway, long story short, I am now the proud owner of a Honda Gold Wing. It cost exactly the price I got for my car. I just need to get my M license. (Yes, you can legally drive a motorcycle with a learner's. Just not very far.) This is number three of the things taking up my time.

No, I haven't written a word except for what I write to you. The last sort of non-purposeful writing I did was back at Uncle Jerry's cabin. It was so dark and depressing, I don't even want to go there. Something about the light at the end of the tunnel going out.

By the way, Camilla tells me I'm a tiger according to the Chinese calendar. We're supposed to be bold and adventurous and bestowed with initiative and charm. However, we have a tendency to be risk takers, making us act before we think about the consequences. And we make good bosses, explorers or racing drivers. Which makes me laugh.

In case you're thinking that Camilla and I are going out, we're not. She's sort of like a big sister to me, which is something I've never had, and gives me deals in exchange for looking after Tyler for a bit here and there. Camilla has taught him to call me Uncle Tiger. I'm not sure why I want you to know that, but I do.

Speaking of sisters, Suzanne actually wrote me a letter (I don't have a phone). It wasn't very long but it reminded me of the look she gave me that day I first left home. She told me mostly about the new dog they got. A Sheltie, called — hold your breath — Scotty. No doubt your great-grandmother would roll her eyes.

Your Snorter sounds a bit like my Camilla, somebody you like but who is totally inappropriate. How come a decent guy like him hangs out with a jerk like your dad? Does he ride a Harley too? Harley owners are basically "snubs" when it comes to bikes. They call my bike a nip bike even though Harley Davidson apparently stole Japanese technology to keep their bikes from leaking oil all over the road. This is what Camilla tells me. She rides a wicked little Kawasaki.

I'm sad to hear about your mom and the kind of crap she puts up with. And blaming you for provoking Gunner is sad too, although you'll have to do it more often if his roars of pain are the result.

But if he's scouting out places in Maine to stash Timmy, then he's more sophisticated than he lets on. Is he? You have quite a garbled household. I may be a bit lonely from time to time, have too much laundry and need a shower, and maybe not eat the way I should, but I'm okay. I'm surviving.

Anyway, these cool May winds are slowly pulling the green from the ground. I've not seen Coyote lately, but I hear him sometimes at night.

I hope your exams go well, as I'm sure they will. You are a very intelligent person. I bet there are scholarships waiting for you.

Take care,

Sween

P.S. Do you have a helmet?

May 23

Dear Sween:

Thanks very much for your letter which came like a good rain at a hard, parched-earth time. I like thinking of you on your Gold Wing. That's a really powerful and comfortable bike. Snorter says you got a great deal there.

Good luck with getting your license soon. And I really admire the effort you are putting into perfecting your pool. I don't think I have either the hand-eye coordination or the confidence to be able to put the spin on a ball, or even to get it to go in a straight line.

Right now it seems that nothing in my life is going in a straight line. I am all "at sixes and sevens" as Great-Granny would say, and "behind like a coo's (cow's) tail."

I am finding it very hard to concentrate on studying for my exams next month. When I think of everything that hangs on getting good marks, my hands get cold and clammy and my mouth goes dry. The idea of sitting down with an examination booklet in front of me seems like the equivalent of facing a firing squad, or the way I imagine you felt before the pool game with the bikers' star player.

I guess I am feeling a bit like you did at your Uncle Jerry's cabin. I keep hoping I will have another dream about my bear to help pick up my spirits.

The fact is I am not getting anywhere in my attempts to change Gunner's mind about Timmy going into a "home." (I am really coming to detest that word.)

Gunner and I had one of our very rare face-to-face "adult conversations" a couple of days ago. I think that has made me even more confused.

I had a free afternoon and I was studying in my room when Gunner knocked on my door and asked if I would come down to the living-room for a "serious talk." Mom was at the salon and Timmy was at school.

I sat on the old maroon armchair and Gunner sat on the couch tapping his finger on the coffee table (usually colonized by his cigarette packages, beer cans and the makings for joints).

I noticed that he had cleared all this paraphernalia away. I also noticed that he seemed straight. He wasn't stoned or hung over. Usually you can tell because his eyelids droop like an elephant's hide and he looks pale around the gills.

I thought he would start in right away about his plans for Timmy. So he really took me aback when he said how sorry he was that things had got so tense and nasty between us over the past few years.

"I want you to know I am really proud of you," he said. "You've got a good brain and I know you are going to make something of your life." I looked at him closely to see if this was some kind of trick. But he looked genuinely sincere.

"I've wasted a lot of chances, Jessica," he said. "You'll be the first one in the family to go to university. And I am every bit as proud of you as your great-granny."

I was still kind of stunned. Gunner hasn't said anything kind to me for at least five years, as best I can remember. So hearing him say "I'm proud of you" was like seeing the lamp in the corner suddenly get up and walk over to me and introduce itself as Fred from Ohio.

Then Gunner did get to the subject of Timmy, as I knew he would. But he put a new spin on it.

"I'm doing this for your sake too, Jessica," he said. "You've got to think of your own future. Do you really want to have to be totally responsible for Timmy if something happens to me and your mother? It's a life sentence, honey."

I could have kicked him when he said that. My eyes started stinging, but I was determined not to cry.

But I could see he really believed what he was saying. He really believes one of the reasons Timmy should go into a home is so that I can be free.

"I want a good relationship with your mother again, Jessica. And she and I can't have that now because of Timmy. So you've got to see that this is the best way for all of us. I know I'm not a patient man. I don't have the know-how for dealing with a kid like Timmy. Neither does your mom. In fact, you seem to be the best at it."

I listened to him, and I felt frozen inside. And the most terrible thing, Sween, was that I could see what he was saying. Because I've thought about the future so often and worried and wondered about how I will manage to help Timmy and still do what I want to do for myself.

And there's truth in what Gunner says. We don't any of us have the know-how. There are times when Timmy is simply unmanageable. When I just want to sit and cry with frustration because he won't listen to me. And because he can't understand at all what I am trying to explain to him — like why he shouldn't run far ahead of me in the mornings to get to the top of the drive to wait for the school bus. Because sometimes he simply isn't careful. He doesn't watch the road for traffic the way I've asked him to time and again, but darts back and forth chasing after butterflies or a bird that's caught his attention.

"I don't want you to have this burden, Jessica," Gunner went on.

And I did start to cry then.

Maybe Gunner thought I was crying because he had finally got through to me and that I was seeing his rationality and his consideration, where before I had seen only cruelty and selfishness.

But I think the real reason I was crying was that I recognized that cruelty toward Timmy in myself. I hated the part of myself that was thinking, "Yes, that's right. Timmy will be a great burden to me. He isn't going to grow out of being autistic. Things will only get harder and harder."

People crying make Gunner really uncomfortable. He did manage to pat my shoulder. And I managed not to flinch.

"Think about what I said. Will you, Jessica?"

And I just nodded.

...

Remember the Jains? The people in India who believe you shouldn't harm the least form of creature life, even inadvertently?

I've been thinking about them a lot these past two days. I've been thinking about how much I love Timmy, and that love requires the kind of selflessness that the Jains work at so hard.

So I am really seriously considering giving up the idea of going to university. That way I can look after Timmy, and Gunner and Mom can go to Costa Rica or wherever.

I've been thinking that I don't need to go to university to be a writer. I know how to read. I know how to look at the world and at the people in it. And maybe that's all you need.

Something else happened — just yesterday — that has made me so confused. And I can't talk about this with anyone.

Except you, Sween.

Here's what happened.

It was Saturday morning and I was feeling pretty low, despite the fact it was a bright, clear day with a fresh wind — the kind of weather I love.

Timmy had been picked up by people from his school who take the kids on special outings every second weekend. Yesterday was a bowling day. Timmy comes back from these outings tired out and happy. (Why can't Gunner see how many things in life Timmy enjoys, and how he is opening up more to people?)

Mom and Gunner were still in bed. I was sitting on the back porch feeling glum, when in roared Snorter on his Triumph Bonneville. I don't think I've mentioned that Snorter has several really classy bikes. You wouldn't necessarily think it to look at him, but he is actually quite well off. His father owned a chain of hardware stores, and Snorter inherited a lot of money when his father died.

Anyway, when Snorter saw how gloomy I was looking, he suggested a trip to Baie-des-Chaleurs.

"You need a break from studying," he said. "And maybe we'll see some seals."

At first I said no thanks. But then I thought, why not? It had been a long, long time since I'd been on the back of a bike, and even longer since I'd seen a seal.

I grabbed one of Mom's helmets (helmets are one thing we have no shortage of in our house) and her leather jacket, and off we went. And I felt really happy riding in the wind behind Snorter's broad back with the world rushing all around us, green and clean and new.

When we got there I just stood watching the waves and the way each crescent sparkled in the sun. I started to feel extremely peaceful and hopeful again as the rhythm of the waves entered my bloodstream and my breathing.

Snorter was looking out at the water and smoking a cigarette.

Then he turned around and looked at me in a really odd way, and he said, "I want you to call me by my real name, Jessica."

I was surprised, and kind of ashamed at the fact I didn't even know his real name. He had always just been Snorter. And then it hit me that he was enunciating all his words clearly. He hadn't fluffed a syllable once since he showed up at the house.

"My name is Stanley," he said. "My mother always called me Stanley. Not Stan."

"Thank you, Stanley," I said, "for bringing me here." And I tried not to smile, because it isn't a name that suits him at all.

Then he started to tell me that I reminded him of his mother, and how much he still missed her even though she died over ten years ago.

"She was a deep thinker like you, Jessica," he said. "And she was thoughtful and quiet, too, and real kind to everyone."

"I'm not that kind," I told him.

"Oh yes, you are," he said. "You just don't see how special and beautiful you are." That's what he said. Special and beautiful. I remember exactly.

And then he kissed me. He kissed me on the lips very softly and it felt wonderful. I don't know how to describe what the feeling was, like a golden electric thrill passing through me.

You are probably thinking, "Poor Jessica. She is so inexperienced and lonely. A little meaningless kiss can get her all excited."

But it didn't feel little or meaningless to me, Sween.

Just then I caught sight of a pair of seals in the bay, their sleek black heads shining as they swam and dove and bobbed about.

APART

"Seals," Stanley said. And for some reason that single word and the way he said it seemed terribly profound, and like a great gift. And then he hugged me and held me close and I can't tell you how warm and safe and strong I felt with his arms around me.

"Don't tell your father, Jessica," he whispered in my ear. "Promise me, on your heart's blood."

I promised, and when I looked up at him again, he had changed. He didn't look Neanderthal any more at all, and I am so sorry now that I ever described him that way.

We got back on the bike and when we got back to Matagouche, Snorter let me off at the top of our drive and took off. He didn't say much. He just smiled and said, "Remember your promise."

Gunner and Mom were just getting up when I got to the house. So they didn't even realize I had gone out.

I think I might be in love, Sween. But I am not sure.

I feel like I've walked through a door I didn't know existed and everything looks different to me now. Everything glows and shines like those seals in the bay.

Or maybe I am just a sad and pathetic odd-looking girl who is excessively grateful for a kind word and a soft kiss.

Maybe it's time to make myself over, give up the university dream and devote the next few years to Timmy's welfare. Maybe it's time I fell in love so that I know what that experience is about, at least.

This confusion is like Great-Granny's sticky treacle, which is a real pain to wipe up when it spills. It's as if I am looking through a window that is clouded over and it's simply impossible to see out clearly. I can't give any shape to my feelings because I am not completely sure I see what they are. I am more confused than I have ever been in my life. Where do I go from here?

Thanks for listening, Uncle Tiger. I hope you are well and happy and that you have your license by the time this gets to you.

Jessica

Dear Jess:

Where do I begin? First off, I'm fine — never better. Went to see my shrink and she's cut my meds in half and thinks my head's finally settling straight on my shoulders.

BUT…what's this about you turning into Mother Teresa all of a sudden (never mind that she's dead) and devoting your life to the woebegone and needy in your household? You realize of course that you are not only taking care of Timmy, but your mother and Gunner as well. I mean that's fine and noble of you but where's your instinct for survival, your creative spirit? How are you going to be able to write (if that's really what you want to do) if you're running around protecting everybody from everybody else? Timmy, if he is healthy, could live another sixty years. And what about you? An old woman picking sea shells by the sea shore? Gunner in his mad fit of decency and humanity has made a lot of good points with respect to your future. (And what is with HIM? Has he found religion or something?)

AND…

Let me get this straight. You are in love with Snorter aka Stanley who is a pool-playing, bike-riding dope dealer living off his dead dad's hardware stores. Now unless YOUR father is caught in some sort of weird time warp, Snorter would be somewhere around his age. I don't care how nice a guy he is, something is definitely wrong with this picture. He can't be all tickety-boo if he goes snorting after his best friend's daughter — no matter how it makes you feel — particularly if he doesn't want you to mention it to your father. No kidding. Gunner'd wrap a bike chain around his neck, drag him behind his bike to the Baie Chaleur and throw his bloody carcass into the briny froth.

If it's a motorcycle ride to the ocean you want, just hang on for a few days. I'll be there.

Yes. In four or five days. Barring mechanical breakdown. I may even beat this letter. I got my license and I want to ride, ride, ride. So I asked Reg if the golf course would survive a couple of weeks without me and if I'd have a job when I got back. He said the frost has stopped heaving the pipes and the heavy grass cutting doesn't really start till the end of June, so have a good trip. Which is exactly what I plan on doing.

I'm packing a tent, sleeping bag, my pool cue (Camilla gave me one that someone abandoned at Cute Ips), a change of clothes and a letter my little sister just sent me. I assume that if I ask around, I'll have no trouble finding your place when I get there.

I'll stop and pick up that mail you sent months ago to see what it said. Tomorrow I hit the road.

See you soon!!

Sween

Dear Suzanne:

As you can see from the postmark, I'm answering your letter from the other end of the country. (I can imagine your blue eyes sitting almost at the edge of your nose because you'd have no way of knowing that I'm gone — unless of course, my boss Reg told Dad.)

At any rate here I am in New Brunswick, a tiny place called Matagouche you can hardly find on a map, visiting a girl/woman Jessica I've been writing to for almost a year. It's been very strange meeting someone you think you really know and then can't be yourself in front of, but I'm sure you don't want to hear the details of my letter life.

I suppose I should have told Mom and Dad that I was taking this trip, but I can count on my little sister to do that for me. Okay?

I'm glad to hear you like your new dog, Scotty. He sounds very smart — certainly more so than dear old Zamboni who I miss a lot. I hope he's not as rude as Boni, if you catch my drift.

I'm also happy to hear you're going into grade nine with

those great marks. And here I thought I got all the brains in the family. (Joke.) High school is a lot different than grade school and you've got to make sure no one pushes you around because now you'll be at the low end of the totem. There's a lot of jerks and creeps and bozos around — and that's just the teachers. Say hi to Mr. Hackles though, if he's still there when you arrive. He's okay. Avoid Mr. Roberts at all possible costs.

Hey! Listen to me giving advice — me, the high school dropout!

I'll try to describe my adventures so far.

The first day I made it all the way to just past Winterpeg. It was pretty windy from the northwest but the bike's so heavy you hardly notice it — except when a truck roars by in the opposite direction, and then it just about throws you off the road. You learn to pull over a bit so the side draft doesn't hit so hard.

I pitched my tent in one of those rest stops you're not supposed to camp in and spent a few hours feeding mosquitoes while I tried to sleep. I was actually glad when some RCMP poked at me to "move along" like I was some sort of hobo or something.

In Kenora I stopped at the post office to see if there was some mail for me C/O General Delivery. And there was! It was from Jessica, the person I'm visiting here. Along with her letter was a money order for $50 which I already gave back. She sent it quite a while ago when I almost left for this trip earlier — the day I wound up on the psych ward, to be specific.

The ride across northern Ontario has got to be one of the boringest in the world. It was okay from Kenora to Thunder Bay — often pretty in fact, with lots of woodsy streams and stuff, but after that it was deadly. And went on forever. And forever. It's totally empty except for rocks and trees and black flies and trucks. Okay, I guess that isn't totally empty, but you get my drift. I didn't think you could fall asleep on a motorcycle, but there were lots of times I had to stop the bike, get off and walk around for a while to wake up — till the black flies started crawling up my nose.

I camped in Wawa one night and it was cold, cold, cold — and noisy. You could hear those trucks screaming down the Trans-Canada for miles. And if it wasn't the trucks, it was the trains.

I was glad to reach civilization, if you can call Sault Ste. Marie civilized. Then Sudbury and North Bay till I hit Pembroke. It's a pretty town with lots of old red brick buildings. It looks like you think Ontario should look — like pictures of old prime ministers.

I didn't even go through Ottawa and Montreal but took side roads as far as I could around them which wound me through the north shore of the St. Lawrence River till Quebec City where it started raining. I never knew how hard it is to waterproof yourself driving down the highway. It's also really hard to see, even when it's not dark. I stayed in a hotel in Rimouski (near where you turn south to N.B.) just to dry off and get a good night's sleep. Except there was a bar below that stayed open till 3 a.m. with a band that played way loud.

Then I think there was a "lady of the night" in the next room plying her trade because strange rhythmic sounds pulsed through the walls long after the band quit. The cleaning lady woke me at 11 a.m. to tell me I had to leave — only she didn't say it in English. But there was no doubt about what she meant.

The funny thing about riding a motorcycle is your IQ drops inversely to the amount of time you spend riding. So by the time I arrived in Bathurst later that night, I was pretty stupid.

I knew Matagouche, my ultimate destination, had to be around some place but I didn't have a clue how to actually find it because my map wasn't detailed enough. So I thought I better ask someone.

This is where the stupid part comes in.

I stopped at a place with a bunch of bikes parked in front — mostly Harleys. Stupid move one. I went inside. Stupid move two. I ordered a beer. Major stupid move three. And then, for the final, ultimate in stupid moves, I played pool.

I don't know if you know but I've been playing quite a lot since I left home and have gotten pretty good, but not nearly as good as I like to think. These two guys insisted on playing for money, but since I kept beating them, I didn't mind at all. On top of that, the cops walked in and wanted to see my ID, but faster than you can say Harley Davidson, these two guys I'm playing with vouch for me and say I'm a long-lost cousin from out west (it doesn't occur to me how they know I'm from "out west" — again the stupid factor at play here) and that I'm with them. (When I say they, I really only mean one guy who played and his buddy who watched it all.) And just when I thought I was invincible, and actually feeling bad for taking all their money, especially after they saved me from the police, and ALL my money was on the table, plus a bunch I didn't even have — they beat me.

I was the victim of the classic hustle.

But just like the amount of time you spend on the bike makes you stupid, the amount of time you spend off it makes you smarter, and I'd been off long enough to just about have my brain back. So as these guys haul me outside to see what my bike is worth, I recognize the tattoo on one guy's arm and suddenly realize this is Jessica's father, a guy by the name of Gunner, and his buddy, Snorter. Jessica looking for her father was how we met, but that's another story and I'll tell you about it some other time.

I tell this guy I know who he is and he says right back to me, "Well I know who you are too, Mr. MacSween. I've been reading the mail you've been sending my daughter."

At this point I just about crap because even though there's been nothing mushy between Jessica and me, our letters have been full of pretty personal stuff, and to know this goon has been reading it makes me feel really sick.

But I owe this guy a ton of money.

So he wants me to do something for him. I won't owe him anything and I can keep my bike if I just do this one little thing. He also warned me that if I say anything to his daughter, he'll do evil things to certain parts of my anatomy. Never mind the details.

I can't tell Jessica any of this. I'm telling you because I want there to be a record of this somewhere and I'm sure you'll put this letter in some safe place (i.e. where Mom and Dad can't find it) in case something happens to me (THEN you can show it to them). But if all goes according to plan, I'll be back home in a week or so — maybe even beat this letter.

At any rate, I better get this in the mail box before Gunner finds it. The best thing for me to do is to play along with his plan (whatever it is) as best as I can — to keep the pressure off Jessica. I'm sorry to burden you like this but I have to tell someone.

Your big brother,

Sweeny

P.S. I'll bring you back a lobster.

Dear Sween:

This is the hardest letter I have ever had to write.

I guess by now you are back in the land of the infinite horizon where the sun looks like God's bellybutton. I hope you got home safely and that both you and the Gold Wing are in good shape.

That is one great bike, by the way, and you are a good person. But I guess it's possible for two good people (and I must hang on to the idea that I am a decent person who wants to be good) not to see eye to eye.

I am still fighting the idea that you betrayed me, Sween. I don't want to think this, but mostly what happened strikes me that way, no matter how often I go over it. I find it horribly painful and confusing to have met you finally, and then ultimately feel let down by what happened between us.

Great-Granny tells me that after you left I couldn't speak for two whole days. I just sat on her couch and cried. I don't remember this at all.

Great-Granny keeps telling me, and I do realize, just how much I have to be grateful for. I will be going to UNB in the fall to study English. And I was absolutely wrong about Gunner's intentions. The home he found for Timmy is the kind of place I dreamed must exist somewhere. The people there are knowledgeable and kind and sensitive. There's a resident speech therapist and a doctor on staff, and the beautiful garden that you saw too, with the big wooden swings. And there's a swimming pool which Timmy loves.

I was amazed at how the man and woman who greeted us managed to put Timmy at ease right away. They even made him laugh. He didn't cling to me or wail or lie on the ground and become an immovable weight. When it was time to go he hugged me and said, "Bye, Juss. I will see you on August 22. Right, Juss?" We'd already fixed on the day. As you now know, Timmy likes to have the exact date that events will occur absolutely fixed in his mind.

So I was the one who blubbed and wanted to lie down on the ground and stay and be close to Timmy.

I can just imagine you reading this and thinking, "So, what is your problem, Jessica? What betrayal are you talking about?"

It's so difficult to put this into words, Sween, because any way I come at it sounds petty, or childishly jealous, or just plain crazy. But I simply can't get rid of this terrible hurt no matter how hard I try to reason with myself.

I keep thinking about the irony of the situation, and how much more secure I felt going down to Maine with Timmy and Gunner, knowing that you were following along behind on your Gold Wing. I knew that if the place smelled filthy or the kids looked sad or hurt, you would help me get Timmy away. You would "spirit him away on the bike if need be," just like you promised.

Knowing you were there helped me endure that awful drive in Gunner's car, sitting with Timmy in the back seat. I understood why Mom stayed home. She was really upset at Timmy going, and we all knew that he would be more comfortable on the journey with just me. But even with the pill Gunner had given him, Timmy was still really restless and anxious.

"Where are we going, Juss? Where?" And I kept saying, "To your new home, Timmy. You'll like it a lot. There's a swimming pool." All the time I was saying those things, I felt like cutting my own tongue out in case I was just parroting Gunner's lies.

It meant so much to be able to look out the back window and see you on the Gold Wing.

And then Gunner decided to stop for a break at a bar. "I won't have a beer, Jessica," he said. "I just need a cold drink and to stretch my legs." Then he added, "Maybe your boyfriend would like a game of pool." I hated the way he said "boyfriend." So I ignored him.

But you didn't ignore him. You were keen to play.

There was a little café across from the bar, remember? That's where Timmy and I went while you joined Gunner.

When you and Gunner came out of the bar together, and I saw his arm around your shoulder and both of you grinning away, I was nearly sick.

Then you said…remember, Sween? You said, "It's all right, Jessica. Gunner says it really is a terrific place he's found for Timmy."

And I couldn't believe what I was hearing. I couldn't believe that you would trust what he told you so unquestioningly.

Then you said the worst thing. You said, "You know, your father's taking care of things the best way he knows how. And I'm helping him."

My heart turned to stone at that instant, a stone that still hangs heavy in my chest. I realize that sounds melodramatic but you looked so changed to me right then. You had become someone I didn't know at all, as if all the letters we had written each other had never existed. I really didn't see how you could possibly think Gunner was taking care of anything, let alone Timmy's needs.

You were suddenly just one of a whole lot of people I have seen in my life who have been absolutely seduced by my father's cruddy charm.

You and Gunner went out together to bars and pool halls in Bathurst. You and Gunner drove up to Baie-des-Chaleurs. You and Gunner went over to Snorter's place to look at his bikes.

Yes, I know. You kept suggesting that I come along. But for me that would have been like drinking poison.

I am sorry to have to write these bitter words to you, Sween. You did so much through your wonderful letters to help me keep going. I really believe we helped each other.

APART

But my father's charisma can put a spell on people. You are not the first to be fooled. It's only that I thought you would be able to see what he really is because of everything I told you in my letters.

I am truly sorry things worked out this way. I will never ever forget the world we had in our letters. Maybe it was the best part of ourselves that wrote those words. The bear and the coyote parts of us were writing, and we saw things by their light for a while.

I will always think of you with the highest regard, Sween. Goodbye and good luck.

Yours very sincerely,

Jessica

From the Fredericton Daily Gleaner, *June 20:*
Archibald William (Gunner) Doig of Matagouche has been arraigned on charges of grand larceny. The theft of two paintings, from the estate of Mrs. Olivia Oliphant of Fredericton, was reported shortly after the disappearance of Mr. Doig who was formerly an employee of Mrs. Oliphant...

September 29

Dear Jessica:

It's taken me quite a while to answer your letter.

I was surprised to hear from you and frankly I didn't know what to say. I decided it was better to wait till I knew your mail was safe from Gunner. Now it's only fair that you know the real truth. Your sense of betrayal is probably even more well founded than you thought, but not for the reasons you suspected. All the same, I am really sorry.

That little clipping you included says it all. I suppose the most important thing for you to know is that Gunner was reading the letters I sent you — or at least some of them. He told me this the night I arrived in Bathurst where we met at Franky's. I didn't know who he was at first — for quite a while actually — but by then I was way in debt to him over several games of pool and that was how it all began. I'll spare you the grisly details.

I wasn't sure what to expect when I arrived in New Brunswick, but whatever it was, it was NOT what I got. I suppose for one thing, I thought YOU might be a little more welcoming. I'm not talking about wild passionate kisses or big hugs, or even little ones for that matter — but some general civility might have been nice. You treated me like something the cat dragged in.

On the other hand, what could I expect? I was so terrified of being civil to you because of Gunner's threats, I must have been pretty icy myself.

My whole perception of everything was turned sideways or upside down by the visit. I didn't expect your mother to be so — how do I put this? — ORDINARY, I guess. I expected someone boozier and frowsier with big dark circles under her eyes — not this quiet, pleasant, smiley attractive woman with bright red hair who seemed interested in everything around her, including me.

I didn't expect Timmy to be as old as he was. You always made him sound like a little kid, not this rather tall ten-year-old. His size alone made him an intimidating presence. Not that he was (is) given to deliberate violence, but he could easily "have an accident" and hurt someone. He does not have the best physical control.

I didn't expect Gunner to be as nasty as you had made him out. But I also didn't expect him to be an artist. Why had you never mentioned that? Simply because he does most of his art on vehicles — he is unbelievably wicked with an airbrush — doesn't diminish the value of what he does. I'm quite amazed at what a snob you are about that. Like if it's not oil on canvas it doesn't count. Just because he's a thief and a jerk doesn't mean he doesn't have talent.

Maybe it's just that he's not all that bright (and maybe his kind of intelligence doesn't register on IQ tests), although it is clear where you get your good looks from. And even if he is not super educated, yes, he can be totally charming. I wish I had some of that charm.

Maybe I'm just jealous, because you certainly had lots of it (charm) for Snorter when he showed up. It was so obvious — him doing his best to ignore you, and you doing the same. And your dad being quite aware of it all. It was hard not to laugh. Or cry.

I didn't expect Snorter to be so young. I thought he'd be your father's age, not 25. He's not much older than us. He is a wizard with a wrench though, and it's a good thing too because Gunner is hopelessly inept at things mechanical — which was a surprise to me. They make a great team. Your dad's art work and paint, and Snorter's wrenching — the total bike-care package. If they lived nearer a city larger than Bathurst, they'd have to beat people away with a stick. And they could name their prices too. But that's not the only thing that your father gets out of the relationship with Snorter. He enjoys tantalizing him with you. I think it gives him some sort of perverse pleasure. And hey, you could do worse. But I don't think an English major would find him interesting for too long.

I did not expect Matagouche to be such a handsome string of middle-class homes hung along the bank of the Matagouche River. I somehow had you clamped up inside a sort of medieval hovel complete with rats and cobblestones. Nothing could have been further from the truth. Modest, yes, but the two-story house with a big veranda at the top end of an acre of fresh-mown lawn is not the picture I got from your dark descriptions of home life. I also didn't know that Bathurst was such an attractive place and that the sea loomed so large on the horizon — very like the prairies.

The only picture you painted with absolute accuracy was that of your great-grandmother Doig (truly a GREAT-grandmother). She was every bit as you described — perhaps even more so. She is certainly never at a loss for words and doesn't care who hears them.

I don't think I got a word in edgewise. Not that it much mattered. She seems to care a lot about you. She certainly noticed how uncomfortable you were with me around.

"What's the matter, Jessica? You're as twitchy as a cat. What's got away?" And that was exactly how you behaved, as though something had escaped you.

And of course I think I know what.

Me. Or your idea of me.

I must have been such a huge disappointment to you, in the first place appearing to get along with your father, and in the second place being so distant toward you. That and being genuinely awkward with Timmy. Of all the things, I'm most sorry about that.

Until, of course, the Paintings Episode.

You know now that the reason I followed you into Maine with Timmy was not simply because it was more or less on the way home, but because I was repaying my debt to Gunner.

I had the paintings on my bike.

Gunner was afraid that because of his past brushes with the law, and despite the fact he was taking his son to Blue Meadow, the border guards/immigration officials might do a strip search of your car. He was certain that a couple of rolled-up canvases carried by an 18-year-old on a motorcycle would barely raise an eyebrow.

And he was right. They didn't search either of us.

What you saw when Gunner and I came out of that small tavern in Maine was the happy conclusion of a deal. And cash for two years of care at Blue Meadow for Timmy. That tavern is a cover for an "import/export" business specializing in high end "collectables."

I knew we were doing something illegal, but I thought it was just smuggling some art work in order to avoid paying duty (wasn't that the whole point of the Free Trade Agreement?). I honestly didn't know the paintings were hot.

So I too have been used and abused by Gunner. I now know what you mean. Except you have to admit that his deceptions do have a Robin Hood aspect about them. I mean it's not like he stole the paintings so he could take a trip to Mexico with another of his girlfriends.

I suppose the only mystery that remains is the identity of the anonymous donor who replaced the funds that were forfeit when the paintings were returned to Mrs. Oliphant. At any rate, I'm glad that Gunner didn't implicate me, in keeping, I suppose, with the dictum of "honor among thieves." Even though I was an unwitting accomplice, I was one.

APART

And now I sit in my leaky trailer wondering about my future. I will not go back to school. I'd rather join Gunner in prison. Strike that. I misspoke myself, as the politicians say. But I will get my grade twelve through correspondence, then maybe take a greenskeeper course, or possibly a mechanic's. One good thing out of all this is I've become a lot closer to my little sister. We get together regularly and Suzanne loves riding on my bike.

I hope you do well at university. I'm sure you will. You'll be comfortable there, and not that far from Timmy.

Maybe I'll do a bit of writing. This is part of something I wrote when I got home.

> But I'd never miss the evening skies
> If I hadn't seen them with your eyes.

The "your" might be you, Juss. It might not. I'll leave it open.

Perhaps when times are brighter and our pasts more distant, we will write again. Maybe we'll even meet each other and see ourselves with the affection and warmth we shared in our letters.

I will miss you. Goodbye.

James Charles MacSween

October 14

Dear Sween:

Thank you for your letter and all its cutting honesty. To be frank, after reading it, I felt as if I had been rolling around naked in broken glass. But that's how the truth feels sometimes, I guess.

Some of your criticisms (of me, for example) are definitely deserved. But other things strike me as just plain wrong.

I am sorry first of all that I was so tense and preoccupied when you showed up. My worries about what was going to happen to Timmy had been building and building, but even more than that, I just felt so extraordinarily hurt when you were so chummy with Gunner right off the bat. I had no idea that you had met him even before you got here and that Gunner was manipulating you and had you over a barrel.

I've been thinking a lot too about your accusation that I'm a snob about Gunner's painting. Maybe that is true. I suppose the whole business of what makes art and literature "good," as opposed to schlock and vulgar is something I'm going to be delving into over the next few years.

I'm still really excited to be here at university in

Fredericton, living in a dorm. I'm meeting new people who care about the same things I do and it's amazing to be able to sit down over a cup of coffee and talk for hours about poems we love. There are times when I get cold feet, and I fear I won't be able to read all these books and write good essays and that I will fail ignominiously. And there are other times when I feel absolutely strong and focused, greedy to learn all I can.

I'm here. I've got a scholarship that covers my next three years. I know I'm lucky.

Gunner, on the other hand, is in Dorchester Pen, where I went to visit him last week. He didn't get bail because he's skipped out on bail in the past. He's still waiting for a trial date, but his lawyer thinks there's a good possibility that a judge will be swayed by the good intentions behind Gunner's theft.

I hope so. I really do. But he'll probably get at least two years.

His spirits are good, actually. He asked about you, Sween, and said how sorry he is that he got you involved in his painting scam. Is he really sorry? Your guess is as good as mine. The good news is that he's talking about improving his reading skills and checking into the literacy programs for inmates.

I hate that word "inmate." I hate the fact that he is in the Pen. I love the idea of what he did and why he did it, although I am extraordinarily sorry he pulled you into it. When I wrote my last letter to you, I had no idea why he stole the paintings. I understand now that's what Stanley meant when he said Gunner's plan to take Timmy down to

Maine "smelled bad." He meant the stupid risk Gunner was taking in order to pay for Timmy's stay in the home.

It's Stanley who is paying now for Timmy to be at Blue Meadow. Remember I told you he inherited a lot of money when his father died? I wonder sometimes if he is doing this because of me. But I believe Stanley always cared about Timmy and I know he would not want to see him suffer in any way.

He really is an extremely kind man, and he was a rock and support for me when I desperately needed it. I am still confused about my feelings for him.

I know that I don't want ever to hurt him or take advantage of him in any way. I also don't recognize at all what you describe as Gunner taking "a perverse pleasure" in tantalizing Stanley with me. Again, maybe this is something I don't want to see, particularly since Gunner and I have had a kind of rapprochement as a result of what you call the Paintings Episode.

He did an illegal and dumb thing for a noble reason, and this has helped me to forgive him for some of his other stupid and cruel actions in the past, especially toward Timmy and my mother.

I don't know why you expected a boozier, frowsier woman. I was sure I had told you that when she is taking care of herself, my mother resembles a flower. Mom is moving down to St. Andrews where she has a job in a spa that specializes in mud packs and baths using kelp gathered on Grand Manan Island.

APART

The old house is to be torn down. Our landlord was apparently not going to renew our lease in any case because he got such a lucrative offer for the land. There's a new housing development going in, and several neat little bungalows will be made to fit on the acreage of the old farmhouse.

I wonder what will happen to the spirits of the children Timmy saw in his room — those happy children of long ago who made him laugh.

I think I've discovered a truth, the real crux of the matter, through writing this letter to you, Sween. Often it works like that for me. Actually writing words down helps to make things come clear in my thinking.

There was another problem between you and me. It wasn't just my (wrong) perception that you had betrayed me through your friendship with Gunner. It was also how you saw Timmy, and I just haven't wanted to confront that directly until now.

Even though there was so much going on when you arrived, I couldn't mistake the shock and dismay — perhaps even revulsion — that I saw on your face when I introduced you to Timmy. I have seen this look on people's faces so often, Sween, and it cuts me to the quick every time. It was that look, and your obvious discomfort when Timmy was around, that made me react to you so coldly on your visit.

I realize now that meeting Timmy must have been really perturbing for you, particularly after you had been spending so much time with Tyler, who is a normal, healthy kid.

Well, as you've seen, Timmy is far from normal. He flaps

his arms about. He ducks his head a lot. He asks the same (rather inappropriate) questions twenty times in a row. I'm sure you didn't need to hear again and again, "Where is Zamboni, Sween?" "Are you sad, Sween?" "Where is Zamboni?"

And of course, even when Timmy is quiet, there is that look in his eyes that is disturbing in itself. He's not here with the rest of us.

I ought to have prepared you better. I ought to have said, "Get ready for a tall ten-year-old who often behaves and talks as if he's two." But I didn't think of that, and then you were suddenly there, looking at Timmy in that way. It's a look that has cruel, unspoken words behind it, like "retarded" and "defective." It's a look that doesn't allow for all the hard-won progress Timmy has made, and all the gifts he has.

I've been thinking how much better it would have been if we'd met face-to-face for the first time in some neutral halfway point, in Kenora or Thunder Bay, without Timmy or Gunner or Mom or anyone else. Just you and me.

That way we could have avoided Gunner getting involved in our lives and jerking us both around. Although it's really ironic when you stop and think of it. It was me looking for Gunner that got you and me connected in the first place. And then when we finally met, it was good old Gunner who helped drive us apart.

I will always be grateful that you and I connected all those months ago, Sween. I think all our letters to each other made a real world, where we were as "present" to each other as two

APART

people can be. I think we had something rare and good.

If you ever want to write to me again, and I've moved from this dorm, you can always reach me through the English Department at UNB.

Your constant friend,

Jessica

P.S. I brought all your letters with me when I moved here.

September 10

Dear Jessica:

I have no idea whether this will reach you because almost a year has passed since I last heard from you, and I'm not certain that the Department of English at UNB will catch your mail. I'm not writing to respond to that letter, mostly because so much in it left me feeling completely helpless in trying to make you understand — understand, for instance, how I really felt about Timmy. But of course there's no point in that. You can't ever "make" anybody do anything.

I assume you're still slogging your way through university and that you continue to do great. School isn't yet showing on my horizon although I read a whole lot. The short version of my Life Since Jessica includes a stint working up north in a uranium mine (kitchen staff) and most recently getting hired on a cruise ship (kitchen staff again).

But the real reason I'm writing is to tell you some stuff of which you may not be aware and should know.

I saved a chunk of money working at the mine and used it to take my little sister Suzanne (not so little now) on a month-long motorcycle trip to the Maritimes. We just got back last week. I wanted to show her some of the sites and sights I saw last year, plus some I never got to see, like the Cape Breton highlands and the Cabot Trail. (The BEST ride in the world, by the way!)

You were on my mind almost the whole way. I wanted to stop and see you, to introduce you to Suzanne, to say hi, to see if we could just "be" together for a bit. We rode by what was your house — no longer there, but a sort of war zone of building and construction. I knew then our meeting would never happen, even though we continued to Fredericton where you presumably are and where we stopped at the Beaverbrook Gallery. I saw that picture you once raved about, the one about Lady Macbeth, and it IS amazing. Suzanne was particularly stunned by it. I was nervous the whole time we were there though, afraid we might bump into you. And I wonder how close we got because I picked up a magazine in the foyer called *Qwerty* because your name was on the cover.

Then we rode to Dorchester and past the penitentiary. I didn't want to see Gunner, just the place he is, the tall thick walls that keep him away from the rest of the world. It looked so incredibly depressing, I almost felt sorry for him, knowing he was inside. But not for long. You'd think that with the passing of time I'd feel more forgiving but I don't.

We stopped at St. Andrews-by-the-Sea (what a beautiful little town!) and I actually saw your mother walking down the street. She saw me, but did not recognize me (I have a beard now — well, part of one) and of course she wouldn't know Suzanne. But we did exchange glances. She looks great. I wish for her sake that Gunner gets out of jail saner.

We got a very nice room at a very grand hotel (the Fairmont Algonquin) and I left Suzanne with cable TV and a hot bath (which she'd been dying for) while I took a day to cross the border into Maine.

Yes, Jessica, I went to visit Timmy. I entered the sunny grounds there, parked my bike and immediately saw an area under some big trees where there was a lot of activity — kids playing, adults watching, helping — just the kind of place you'd expect to find Tim. I suppose I should have formally checked in at the entrance, but I didn't. I wandered across the lawn toward the shade where a small group was playing some sort of game with a ball. But off to the side sitting alone cross-legged in front of one of those trees was a boy wearing a white helmet. I was certain it was Timmy. He sat there, nodding back and forth.

As I approached him, a guy about my age approached me. He was staff. He wore a tag that said Wayne something.

"Can I help you?" he asked. He was polite. He had an open face.

"Yes, I came to see him," I said. "I'm a friend of the family."

"Oh," said Wayne. "He's not having a good day. We've had to put a helmet on him because he keeps banging his head. Hey, buddy," he called gently, "you've got a visitor. It's…what's your name?"

"Sween."

"Sween's here to see you."

It was awkward trying to get around the tree and crouch to see his face to talk straight to him.

APART

"Timmy, it's me, Sween," I said.

"What did you call him?" asked Wayne.

"Timmy."

"That's not Timmy. That's Allen. Timmy's off swimming today with another group."

A great tsunami of relief mixed with embarrassment rolled over me. I was too stunned to speak.

"They'll be back around supper time, if you want to wait."

"No, I've got to get back to my sister. She's waiting for me in St. Andrews. But would you tell him that Sween was here to see him? Just say Sween and Zamboni, my dog."

"I'll tell him. He's doing really well. He has a sister…" I couldn't tell if he paused here because he was trying to recall your name, or whether he was reliving a moment with you.

"Jessica," I prompted.

"Yes, Jessica — *the poet*. She visits him often. His mother too."

He didn't say "the poet" as though he'd underlined it. That was me. He said it as though it was part of your name.

When I got back to St. Andrews, I opened that copy of *Qwerty*, and in it I found this:

> …if I turn too suddenly
> I can see how all those worlds
> came together then fell
> apart
> in the blink of an I.
>
> — *Jessica Doig*

{175}

And that is what I wanted you to know.

So now we have come full circle. I began this whole thing by writing you first. Now I'm ending it. Please don't write back. It wouldn't be possible anyway since I'll soon be floating somewhere between St. Lucia and the Bahamas.

Perhaps we'll meet again in another life.

As ever, your lost friend,

James Charles MacSween

DATE DUE

12/15/09		
12 4 JAN 20		
2 7 NOV 20		
The Library Stor		